# THE CORNUDAS GUNS

**Center Point
Large Print**

**This Large Print Book carries the
Seal of Approval of N.A.V.H.**

# RAY HOGAN

# THE CORNUDAS GUNS

CENTER POINT PUBLISHING
THORNDIKE, MAINE

The text of this Large Print edition is unabridged. In other
aspects, this book may vary from the original edition. Printed in
Thailand. Set in 16-point Times New Roman type by
Bill Coskrey and Gary Socquet.

ISBN 1-58547-340-5

Library of Congress Cataloging-in-Publication Data

Hogan, Ray, 1908-
    The Cornudas guns / Ray Hogan.--Center Point large print ed.
      p. cm.
    ISBN 1-58547-340-5 (lib. bdg. : alk. paper)
    1. Large type books.  I. Title.

PS3558.O3473C67 2003
813'.54--dc21

2003048880

*to my friend*
JAMEY CREAGER
*of Salem, New Mexico*

# 1

JAKE BENEDICT felt the sheriff's cold, hostile gaze rake him from hat to boot. It wasn't an uncommon welcome. He had been accorded a like greeting in many of the towns he had passed through since leaving Tennessee—some of which had made it abundantly clear that they had no use for drifters.

Such had irked Jake Benedict at first. He was no down and out saddlebum looking for a handout, or for trouble. Far from it; he was a man with a serious purpose in mind, and while at the beginning of the journey back in the Cumberland Gap-Powell River country of Tennessee he may have looked like one of the thousands of fiddle-footed, flat-broke longhairs roaming the land, he had fairly well corrected that impression in both dress and manner by the time he reached the Texas border.

There he had also made other changes. It had become apparent the aged bay horse he was riding was in no condition to travel any farther. The gelding had been the best of the general use farm stock he'd had, and when he sold off the place shortly after his mother's death, he had hung onto the bay for personal needs.

The gelding had held up well all the way across Tennessee and Arkansas, but by the time they had crossed into Texas it was evident the bay was finished. Benedict had reluctantly traded his old friend, along with the creaky McClellan army saddle his father, Fritz, had brought home after the close of the war, for a younger horse, also a bay, and more suitable gear. Jake likewise rid himself of the pack mule that he'd trailed long, deeming the animal no longer necessary.

It had been a long, tiresome ride, almost a month and a half, from the farm to the settlement in New Mexico territory where he hoped to find his father. But hope was about all the assurance he had. Fritz Benedict had ridden away well over three years ago, not actually abandoning his wife and son, but heading west in search of a better life for all. Things just never seemed to work out right for him in Tennessee, and he was sure all would change once he reached the new frontier and got settled. Once that was accomplished he would send for them.

They had had no word from Fritz Benedict for a full year, and then a letter arrived telling them that he was still searching for his dream. He was intending to try his hand at prospecting for gold in the Colorado Rockies, near a town called Cripple Creek, and if his and his partner's luck was good, he would have more than enough to bring them west and start a new life in high style.

That letter had come from a town in Colorado called Garland City. The next word Jake and his mother had received was postmarked Las Vegas, Territory of New Mexico, and reached them a year later. Fritz was on his way south to a settlement called Las Cruces, which was not far from the Mexican border. He expected to locate on some of the free land nearby and get into raising horses. There were several army forts in the area, all of which were good markets for horses—"remounts" Fritz had termed them—and in no time at all, with the United States government as well as ranchers in the vicinity as steady customers, he would be able to make his fortune.

Jake, and his mother Emma, had heard no more from Fritz after that letter, and both had assumed he was proceeding with his plans. Fritz was always one to have grand ideas, both Jake and his mother realized, but beneath his daydreaming a streak of practicality shone through, and this time it did appear that he was on the right track. The family would be reunited soon now, both thought, and so they continued their lives on the farm with a bated air of expectancy.

But as the weeks slid into months, and another year passed with no further word from Fritz, Emma's health declined, lung fever overtook her, and she died. The loss was a numbing shock to Jake, just as he knew it would be to his father when the word reached him.

As could be expected Jake lost all interest in the farm after the death of his mother, and the following spring cast about for a buyer of the property, and quickly sold out. He was determined now to go west himself to the town in New Mexico territory called Las Cruces—The Crosses someone had said it meant in the Spanish language—to find his father and join him.

Jake had the money paid him for the farm, not a large amount to be sure as farm land wasn't worth much. But there'd be enough to help Fritz in his horse-raising venture, and maybe make things easier for him.

They could work together, Jake figured. He was a pretty good hand with horses, knew how to look after them, train them, even doctor them when they came down with some ailment. He had had plenty of experience along such lines while running the farm. Fritz should welcome him as a partner. Together with his father's friendly personality and his own knowledge of stock, they should be able to really make it big raising horses.

And the moment when he would see his father again after so long a time, after so much had happened, was drawing nearer. He had felt a lift within him as he rode out of the needle-spired mountains folks called the Organs and headed for the settlement of Las Cruces; soon he would be united with his father, and they could then begin a new life together.

It looked like good country, Jake thought as he followed the road paralleling a river called the Rio Grande—much different from much of that he had just crossed, which had been covered with dry sand, weeds, cactus, and other lifeless-looking growth. Around Las Cruces there was green grass, and big trees, and wild flowers to be seen.

His mother would have liked the area, he felt certain, but she wouldn't have had anything of a complimentary nature to say about the country that lay in between the Cumberland Mountains and the New Mexico settlement. She would have missed grassy hillsides, valleys with clear, running streams, and heavily leafed trees, but most of all she would have missed people.

The West was a vast emptiness. Towns were few and very far apart. There were no farms lying at neighborly distances, only scattered ranches that usually were miles from habitation of any sort. And those who lived on the land were different; most were the silent, suspicious kind, slow to warm to strangers, slower yet to become a friend. But Emma Benedict had been spared all that. Born and raised in the Cumberland country where a person knew everyone, or perhaps was even related, she would never be subjected to the cold-shoulder receptions he had encountered many times along the way.

Too bad, though, that she had not lived to see Las Cruces, Jake thought as he rode into the town. It offered all the things she liked—stores, homes, churches, even a hotel along with all the other things that went to make life pleasant. All such reflections had vanished from Jake Benedict's mind, however, by the time he had located the town's jail, had pulled to a halt before it, and swung from his saddle.

In his mid-twenties, he was not a tall man, but one just slightly above average. Of muscular build, with thick shoulders, he had dark hair in need of trimming at the moment. His eyes were light, as his mother's had been, but he had the blocky facial features of his father. Dressed in tan, canvaslike pants, faded red shirt, flat crown brown hat, and scarred stovepipe boots, he looked to be just what he was—a man who had spent his life until then on a farm.

He had no holstered pistol at his side; he instead carried a well-worn Henry repeating rifle in one hand, and a bandolier of cartridges slung across his shoulder. Leaning the weapon against a leg, Jake drew a red bandanna from his hip pocket, mopped at the sweat glistening on his sun brown face and neck, and glanced about at the people taking note of him and the dusty bay he was riding. The heat was extreme, but it was August and he reckoned there was little difference on that score between Tennessee and New Mexico.

Aware of the hostility in the man who had appeared suddenly in the doorway of the jail to mark his arrival, Jake nodded slightly and produced a wry smile.

" 'Morning, Sheriff. Mighty hot around here . . . You happen to know a man named Fritz Benedict? He's—"

The features of the lawman, a dark, heavy man with small, deep-set eyes and a crown of white hair, had abruptly stiffened.

"Know him!" he shouted before Jake could finish. "You bet I know him! Me and the army both have got men out right now hunting the thieving bastard!"

## ⟿ 2 ⟿

JAKE BENEDICT'S features tightened. His eyes narrowed and his shoulders lifted slightly as sudden anger shot through him.

"That's mighty strong talk," Jake said coldly. "What's it mean?"

"Means this here Fritz Benedict you're asking about is an outlaw—the worst damned kind—that's what it means. And if I could get my hands on him I'd see him hang just as fast as I could get him up before a judge."

Jake, shock holding him rigid and tight-lipped, shook his head. "What did he do?"

The lawman brushed at the sweat on his face, and then ran stubby fingers through his hair. He wore his gray-streaked black mustache handlebar style, and the stubble of beard on his cheeks and chin bore evidence to the fact that he'd been too busy in the past few days to use a razor.

"Held up a freight wagon loaded with guns for the army, that's what. Aims to sell them to the Apaches. Ain't nothing worse'n a white man who'll sell—"

"You sure of that?" Jake broke in quietly, the disbelief in his tone apparent.

"Sure as my name's Eli Dirksen," the lawman snapped. He glanced about. Several men moving along the street nearby had paused to stare and listen. Again swiping at the sweat on his face, he came back to Jake. "Now you answer a question for me. Why are you so damned interested in him?"

"Happens my name's Benedict, too—Jake Benedict."

"Fritz Benedict some kin to you?"

"My pa's name is Fritz."

Dirksen's jaw hardened. "Is that a fact," he said loudly. The men close by drew nearer. "What are you hunting him for? You going to throw in with him, that it?"

"I figure to join him, if that's what you're saying," Jake replied. "Understood he had a ranch around here somewheres—a horse ranch."

A buggy wheeled by, driven by a man sitting ramrod straight on the seat. The young woman beside him was pretty with dark hair and large, wide-placed eyes. Jake caught her curious glance, returned it indifferently.

"A horse ranch—Fritz Benedict!" the lawman said with a laugh. "You're joshing me, friend."

Jake shrugged. "Man you're talking about can't be my pa. He'd never get mixed up in holding up a freight wagon or a stage, something like that."

"Name of the jasper I'm talking about is Fritz Bene-dict—which you claim is the name of your pa. Now, whether they're the one and the same I ain't got no way of knowing. What's your pa look like?"

"Been close to four years since I last saw him so I don't know exactly. Was about the same height as me. Had dark hair—"

"Hell, in four years a man could change to look like nobody you'd ever seen," Dirksen said, glancing at the crowd for approval. There was no audible response, but Jake sensed a rising hostility directed at him by the onlookers.

The buggy with the pretty girl and the rancher was turning into a stable a short distance down the street; Carson's Livery Barn, Jake saw, reading the faded sign on its high facade.

"I'm wondering about you a mite," Benedict heard the sheriff say. The lawman now leaned against the wall of the building, thumbs hooked in the pockets of his leather vest. "I'm thinking maybe you come to throw in with your pa, be his partner—and I sure don't mean in raising horses."

"That's how it would be, Sheriff, no matter what you think," Jake said evenly. "How long has this man you're looking for been around here?"

"Three, maybe four days—"

Jake shook his head, relieved. "Can't be my pa. Letter we had from him, maybe a year ago, said he was coming down here then to get started ranching. He would have been here a lot longer'n three or four days."

"How do you know for sure? Seems to me a man

that's been gone from his family as long as you say he has, and that you ain't heard from for a year or so, is plenty unreliable. You can't be sure he come down here. He could have told you that, intending to, then changed his mind and went somewheres else."

Benedict silently admitted the possibility, but he was stubbornly unwilling to accept it. "There any other towns close by where he might've settled?"

"El Paso's about forty miles south. There's some other towns scattered about but Las Cruces is the main one. Be here where your pa would've come, I expect—and far as I'm concerned, did. Only it wasn't no year ago he got here. Was maybe a week . . . If this jawboning's going to keep on, let's step inside my office, out of the sun."

Dirksen, without turning, backed into the room behind him, and settled into the chair placed at a table that served as a desk. The office was small, sparsely furnished with two benches along one of the bare walls. A door off another wall apparently led to the jail area. It was hardly any cooler inside the building, but it was out of the driving sun, and away from the crowd that had continued to grow.

"The holdup of that freight wagon take place around here?" Benedict asked, still hoping to find proof that a mistake was being made, that it wasn't his father.

"Nope, was out at the Cornudas way station east of here about sixty miles. Benedict hung around there for a couple of days, then left when the freighter come in. Like I said, it was carrying guns—fifty new-fangled repeating rifles along with a thousand rounds of ammunition. Army was supposed to do some experimenting with them.

"Benedict waited until the wagon pulled out. Was only the driver and the shotgun on the seat. He jumped them when they was a couple of miles from the station—killed them both. The shotgun didn't die right off, however, and was able to tell Cal Hollenbeck, the station agent, who the hijacker was."

"He outright say it was Fritz Benedict?"

"I reckon he did—named him straight off to Hollenbeck. The shotgun had seen him hanging around the livery stable, and Gus Underwood's saloon, right here in town."

Jake was conscious of the lawman's eyes drilling steadily into him as he turned slightly and looked out into the street. The crowd had broken up and drifted away, and well off in the distance somewhere a dog was barking insistently.

"I keep doing some thinking about you," Dirksen said, "and I'm getting the notion that maybe I'd be smart to lock you up until we run down this Fritz Benedict."

A hard smile parted Jake's lips as he leaned back against the door facing. "I ain't much where the law's concerned, Sheriff," he drawled, "but I know you have to charge a man with something before you can do that—and you don't have anything on me."

"You've got the same name as the man me and the army are hunting for—and you're saying yourself you figure he's your pa."

"Name's the same, but it ends there. I don't think the man you're after is my pa."

Jake spoke with what he believed was conviction but in his heart he was far from certain. He could not conceive of his father being guilty of such a crime—hijacking rifles and ammunition from a freighter and selling them to the Apache Indians. But things seemed to add up and point in that direction.

Dirksen stirred angrily, then spat at a lard bucket cuspidor placed alongside the potbellied stove. "No, reckon I can't throw you in a cell just because your name's the same . . . Dammit all, I don't see why the hell this didn't happen across the line in Texas! That's where them guns was headed for anyway—Fort Bliss. Then it would've been up to the Texas Rangers to handle it. But, no, hijacking went and took place in New Mexico, in my county, so it's up to me."

"You've got men out looking for this man. Expect they'll turn him up?"

"Yeah, me and the army both's got posses out, but they sure ain't had no luck yet, and they've been combing the country ever since it happened." The lawman paused, studied Jake thoughtfully. "What are you aiming to do next?"

Jake shrugged. "Try to find my pa, if he's around somewhere, and straighten out this mess—prove to you and everybody that he ain't the one who hijacked the guns. Think I'll talk to the livery stable owner, Carson, and maybe to that saloonkeeper—"

"Gus Underwood," the sheriff supplied when Jake hesitated. "Doubt if they can tell you much more than I have, but suit yourself."

"Thought maybe this Fritz Benedict might've dropped

a word or two about his family, or where he was from. Could tell from that whether he's my pa or not."

"Yeah, you could at that. One thing, folks around here ain't got no use for any man that'll deal with the Apaches. Most of them lost friends or relatives at some time or another before the army settled the critters down, and if they figured you might have something to do with stirring them up again, and putting them on the warpath—well, I sure can't be responsible for what might happen to you."

"From what I heard back up the road a few days ago the Indians are already pretty much stirred up," Benedict said. "Was told one of the chiefs over in Arizona—Victorio they called him—was getting the tribes together, and aiming to drive the whites out of the country."

"Was told about that, too. Victorio is a bad one, and he's always caused a lot of trouble. Our Mescaleros are peaceful—leastwise they have been. But if some of the young bucks kick over the traces and pay no mind to their chief, Cobre, then we'll have a problem. The army figures they'll be the ones your pa'll be selling them guns to."

"You don't know it's my pa—and I'm plenty sure it ain't," Jake said quietly.

"Maybe, but what I'm saying is if them young bucks get their hands on them new repeaters and all that ammunition it'll be hell to pay around here."

Jake nodded his understanding as Dirksen, leaning forward with his elbows on the table, considered him closely. The attitude of the lawman had changed; he was now considerably less antagonistic than he'd been at the start.

"Still ain't sure about not locking you up—for your own good."

"You sure it's for my protection or is it because you still figure I might be going to join up with my pa in selling those rifles?" Jake said, a half smile on his face.

"Maybe a little of both," Dirksen said, and began to thumb through a sheaf of papers on his desk. "Want you to stick around town for a few days—leastwise until my men or the army nails this Benedict. Know then for sure whether you're mixed up in it."

"I'll keep that in mind, Sheriff," Jake said. He turned into the doorway, stepped out onto the landing, and crossed to the hitch rack where his horse was waiting. Then, swinging up into the saddle, he pointed the bay for Carson's Livery Stable.

Letty Kellen, sitting beside her father Tom as they rode down the main street of Las Cruces for Carson's, took note of the man speaking with Sheriff Dirksen in front of the jail. He was a stranger, she was certain of that for although she was not in the settlement more than three or four times a month—the family ranch being some twenty-five miles east—she knew he was not one of the regular, ordinary cowhands that one found in the town.

"Get your trading done in a hurry, Letty," she heard her father say in his commanding, autocratic, no-quarter voice. "I'll be ready to head back for home in an hour—no more'n that."

"All right, Papa," Letty replied, for once not feeling a stir of resentment at his manner. Tom Kellen was a good man, but one who felt he was lord of all, and was inclined to let the world in on that fact at every opportunity. "I'll be at the livery stable."

"See that you are. The drive to the ranch is a long one and I don't hanker to be out on the flats after dark—not with the Apaches acting up like they are."

"All right, Papa. I'll be waiting at Carson's."

She really didn't have any particular shopping to do. It was just that she was bored with having so little to do around the ranch since her father had reached the point where he could hire people to get everything done. Even the kitchen chores were now handled, since the death of her mother, by a Mexican woman named Filomena.

Each day it was a matter of finding something to keep herself busy, something with which to occupy her time. She did do quite a bit of riding, and helped the cowhands when there was stock to be moved or branding to be done. Now and then she'd even go off into the brakes where it wouldn't bother anyone and practice shooting with the rifle her father had given her.

Letty supposed she ought to be happy and contented with her life, but admittedly she was not. Once she had finished school in Las Cruces she seemed to lose all contact with the friends she'd made. Many of the boys and girls she'd associated with lived on ranches also, but the one closest to her father's Rocking K was a long thirty miles away. And there was nothing in Las Cruces of interest other than things to buy, and she was weary of that.

She should be finding herself a husband, her father had told her on several occasions in his blunt, direct way. She would be happy to comply if ever the right man came along. But she could never get interested in the cowhands or any of the other ranchers' sons that she met in the settlement or at the periodic schoolhouse dances that she attended now and then. So when her father got too insistent she usually was able to shut him up by saying that she never expected to find a man of whom he'd approve.

Letty glanced up. They had reached the stable and were wheeling through the wide, sliding door into the runway. She glanced quickly over her shoulder toward the jail—more in a gesture of curiosity than anything else, she assured herself. The stranger was still there in conversation with Sheriff Dirksen. Letty couldn't account for the interest the stranger aroused in her other than the fact that he was new in town; she admitted, however, that he had drawn her attention as no other man ever had.

"Remember now—one hour," Tom Kellen said, lifting his lean shape off the buggy seat and dropping to the ground.

"I'll be here and ready, Papa," Letty said, and watched him square his high-crowned, peaked hat on his head and hurry off down the dusty street to transact whatever business it was that had brought him to town.

"Anything I can do for you, Letty?"

Rufe Carson's question drew the girl's attention. She had been looking beyond the departing figure of her father—so erect and inexorable in his sharply creased black trousers, crisp white shirt, red string tie, polished boots, and tall hat—to the jail once again. The stranger was no longer on the landing, apparently having moved on. A pang of disappointment stirred through her as she looked down.

"Letty? There something bothering you?"

At the anxious tone of the stableman's voice Letty looked up. She shook her head. "No, just thinking about something. I guess I'd better get my shopping done," she added and came down from the buggy without accepting Carson's proffered hand. "I'll be back shortly."

Rufe Carson, a squat, dark man in overalls, and thick-soled shoes, nodded. "You can wait in the office," he said. "Got all the windows open. It's a mite cooler in there."

"Thank you," Letty said as she walked up the runway to the door.

She wanted to ask Carson if he knew who the stranger she'd seen talking to the sheriff might be, but the notion passed. He was probably just another drifter who would be gone before the day was over.

⟶⟹ 3 ⟸⟵

Y OU CARSON?" Benedict asked as he rode into the runway of the livery barn and halted before the man who faced him.

"Reckon I am," the stable owner replied. "What can I do for you?"

Jake swung down from the saddle. Carson, hands jammed into the pockets of his overalls, studied him closely, almost suspiciously, Benedict thought—and that could be an indication there was a resemblance between him and the man involved in hijacking the army's rifles.

"Name's Benedict. The sheriff told me you—"

"You some kin to Fritz Benedict?" Carson, bristling instantly, cut in.

Jake pulled off his hat and brushed away the sweat beading on his forehead with the back of a hand. He was enjoying the odors of the livery barn—the smells of horses, of leather, of fresh hay. It reminded him of home, of the farm back in Tennessee—of that other life.

"Not sure," he said finally. "My pa's got the same name, but I sure don't think he's the man the law and the army's after."

Rufe Carson leaned back against the partition that separated the first stall from the second in the runway. The stable was near empty, Benedict saw; only the horse and buggy he'd seen pass when he was in front of the jail talking to Dirksen were in evidence.

"Well, he's the only Fritz Benedict I ever come across," the stableman said testily. "Expect he's your pa all right. What about him?"

"Understood he hung around here a bit—"

"No more'n he did Underwood's saloon," Carson snapped. "You trying to say he was a friend of mine?"

"No, only trying to find out if he was my pa, and where he might be."

"Now, just where in the hell do you think a man who'd just stole himself a wagonload of guns and bullets and was aiming to sell them to the Indians, would be? Not around here for damn sure! He'd be off getting things all set with the Indians."

Carson's anger flooded his features, and his mouth worked spasmodically. Benedict waited out a long minute for the man to recover himself, and then smiled.

"You're right—and I didn't mean it to sound that way. Like I told the sheriff, my pa came down here to start a ranch and raise horses. I don't figure he got himself mixed up in hijacking a lot of rifles. Not that kind of man."

"Well, it was a Fritz Benedict that done just that," Carson stated flatly. "One of the men he murdered was a good friend of mine, and he seen him plain."

"Sheriff told me that—"

"Then what are you digging for? Can't be no doubt far as I'm concerned."

Jake's temper was rising steadily. The stableman's attitude was even more unreasonable than that of Eli Dirksen.

"Just trying to come up with something that'll tell me for sure whether it was my pa that took the guns. I don't figure it was."

"Figure all you want, but you ain't going to worm him out of it. And there ain't nothing I can tell you. He stabled his horse here for one—no, maybe it was two nights—a bony, spavined-looking little black mare. Didn't want nothing done to the animal 'cept feeding and stabling—and that wasn't because he was broke. Paid me from a poke that looked to have quite a bit of cash in it."

"You think he might have had a shack around here close—the starting of a ranch, maybe?"

"Misdoubt that," Carson said, pausing to fill and light

his pipe. "That posse Dirksen's got riding and the army patrol that's out would have come across it."

"Seems they would have," Jake agreed. "Noticed you looking me over real sharp when I rode in. You see some resemblance in me to the man you call Fritz Benedict?"

Carson puffed thoughtfully on his pipe. "Well, maybe yes and maybe no," he said as he considered Jake. "You're about the same build, I reckon. Can't tell you how he looked in the face because he was wearing a thick beard."

"He happen to mention where he was from?"

"Nope, sure didn't. Wasn't much for looking after his horse, can say that. Animal was in bad shape—like it had come a far piece. When I mentioned he ought to do something about it told me he wasn't aiming to keep the animal much longer . . . Where was your pa when you last heard from him?"

"Place called Las Vegas—up in the northern part of the territory."

"How long ago was that?"

"Year or so. He was in Colorado before that, prospecting for gold. Letter that come from Las Vegas though said he was heading down this way, to Las Cruces. Figured to start raising horses."

Carson removed his pipe from between his yellowed teeth, and shook his head. "Horses are my business. If some fellow started raising them around here anywhere close I'd've heard about it—and I sure never did. Expect he changed his mind, decided there was a easier way to make money."

Benedict ignored the implication, and made no comment. What the stableman said was logical, but Jake was still unwilling to admit that his father had become an outlaw.

"Could be you—" he began, and checked his words. The girl he had seen in the buggy was entering the stable, apparently coming for the rig.

"Howdy again, Letty." Carson greeted her with a big smile. "All done with your store trading?"

"All finished," she answered, touching the small package under her arm. "I see Papa's not here yet."

Jake could feel the girl's eyes on him, making a frank appraisal. They were light blue under dark brows, and in the muted light of the stable, her hair appeared to be black. She was wearing an ankle length, light brown dress, with a lace collar and a pert straw hat held in place with a jeweled pin.

"No, ma'am, not yet," Carson said, "but he'll be coming pretty quick. Now, you just make yourself to home in my office. Got all the windows open. Be a mite cooler there."

"Thank you, Rufe," Letty said. Then she nodded to Jake and added, "You must be a stranger in town. I thought I knew everyone around here—the ones my age, anyway."

"Just sort of passing through," Benedict said.

Letty had a somewhat lower voice than expected of a woman, he noted, and she was much prettier than he'd thought at first look. When she smiled, as she was doing now, small lines gathered at the corners of her eyes which seemed to have dancing lights in them.

"I'm Letty Kellen. My father has a ranch about

twenty-five miles east of here," the girl said, and extended her hand.

"His name's Benedict," Carson volunteered before Jake could speak. "He's looking for his pa."

The expression on Letty's face changed as Jake took her hand—not to one of hostility as had been evident on others, but to a sort of regret and disappointment.

"Benedict. Isn't that the name of the man who held up that freight wagon and killed those men?"

"Sure is. Fritz Benedict," the stableman said. "Jake here don't think it was his pa, but the name's exactly the same."

"Still don't think the hijacker was my pa," Jake said as Letty drew back a step. A frown pulled at her evenly tanned features.

"I see," she murmured. "But if the name is the same, and your father is around here, why—"

"I don't think pa could do what this man did, kill two men and make off with those rifles. He was always kind, easygoing and—"

"He ain't seen his pa in years so he plain wouldn't know nothing about what he'd be like today," Carson said, again quick to speak up. "He don't seem to realize how much a man could change in all that time."

Silence fell between them after that, broken only by the restless stirring of a horse somewhere in the rear of the stable, and the distant rapping of a hammer.

"Why are you looking for him around here?" Letty asked, breaking the hush. "Seems this would be the last place you'd find him."

"His pa—" Carson began, but Benedict waved the

27

man to stillness.

"I can do my own talking," he said. "Had a letter from him saying he was moving down here to start raising horses. I figured to throw in with him and—"

"I ain't heard of nobody starting a horse farm any-where around here, Letty, have you?" Carson cut in.

The girl's attitude had altered somewhat, and she was again cautiously friendly. "No, I haven't." Then nodding to Jake, she started toward the rig standing in the runway. "I'll wait for Papa in the buggy. It's not too hot, and I'm sure he'll be along shortly."

Benedict watched her move off, a sort of reluctance passing through him. He would like to be friends with her, and the possibility had been present at first, but the mention of his name had changed all that. She was now coolly polite and distant.

"You got any more questions you want answered?" Carson's flat voice broke into Benedict's thoughts.

Jake shrugged. What few he had asked had brought forth little if any helpful information. "No. Think I'll go have a few words with Underwood at the saloon. The sheriff said this Fritz Benedict—"

"You mean your pa—" Carson cut in pointedly.

"Said this Benedict hung around his place a bit, too," Jake finished, ignoring the interruption. Turning to his horse, he grasped the saddle horn and reins and swung up onto the bay's back. "Obliged to you for your time," he said as he settled himself. Then with a final glance at Letty Kellen sitting stiffly upright in her buggy, he cut the horse about and returned to the street.

Underwood's saloon, only a few strides down the way,

was all but deserted at that late morning hour. Entering the low, flat-roofed, adobe structure Jake sought out the bartender and inquired about the owner. He was directed to a slight, middle-aged man relaxing in a chair at the back of the room.

"I'm Jake Benedict," he announced, halting before Underwood. "Was told you got acquainted with a man going by the name of Fritz Benedict."

Underwood removed the cigar he was smoking from between his lips, flicked the ashes on the floor, and, cocking his head to one side, said, "So?"

"Trying to locate him—see if he's my pa, the real Fritz Benedict."

Underwood, dressed in a wrinkled, somewhat stained white suit, equally soiled white shirt, and black string tie, shrugged. "Fritz Benedict I knew held up a freighter, killed the driver and the guard, and got away with about fifty new rifles and a big supply of ammunition."

"I've heard all that," Jake said patiently, "and I'm saying again that I don't think it was my pa, but somebody else using his name."

"Ain't likely," Underwood said dryly. "That ain't a name a man hears on every corner. What do you want from me?"

"Was wondering if you did much talking to Benedict," Jake replied, and asked questions similar to those he'd put to Sheriff Dirksen and stable owner Carson. No, Benedict had never mentioned where he was from nor talked about his family, Underwood said, and he'd never mentioned anything about going into raising horses. The saloonman had then finished the conversation with a warning.

"Ain't sure how to figure you, Benedict. Could be you're all right, and could be you're in here to throw in with your pa. Whatever. I'd be mighty careful about telling folks who you are if you aim to go around asking questions. The whole country's jumpy about the Apaches raising hell again, and if you're the son of the man selling them guns—well, I'd sure not want to be in your boots."

"Wasn't my pa—" Jake began and let it drop. There was no use in trying to convince anyone that his father could not be involved in such a crime; they just wouldn't believe him. A name was a name—and that was all the proof they required.

Of course, it was possible his father was guilty; Jake Benedict had to admit that again to himself. He'd never been very close to Fritz, the drudgery of continual hard farm labor always being a detriment to their becoming close. Add to that the years that had passed since he'd seen his father, and you came up with the fact that he actually knew very little about Fritz Benedict. The man who had hijacked the Cornudas guns could very easily be his father—or it could be an entirely different person. Regardless, Jake had to know for sure one way or another—else he'd never have a moment's peace of mind.

"This way station where the holdup took place, how do I get there?" he asked, bringing his attention back to Gus Underwood. The saloonman was still studying him closely as he sucked on his cigar. Elsewhere in the shadowy room there was relative quiet among the three or four patrons.

"Take the road leading south out of town, follow it till you come to the forks, then bear left," the saloonman said, and outlined further directions.

"How far is it?"

"Sixty miles, more or less."

That would run into two days' travel, Jake realized, considering that it was now almost noon. But that was where he should go to start his search for his father. He'd learned nothing worthwhile here in Las Cruces other than that Fritz Benedict was a wanted, and much hated, man—and that the hate was spilling over onto him. The hell with that. He reckoned he could live with what other people thought of him, at least until he could straighten things out.

"Obliged to you," he said to Underwood, and retraced his steps through the saloon to the hitch rack where the bay gelding waited. He'd get himself a bite to eat at the restaurant he'd noticed down the street, and then head for the Cornudas way station. Maybe his luck would be a little better there.

══ 4 ══

JAKE enjoyed a fine meal in a restaurant called the Busy Bee. While there he had a lunch of meat-and-bread sandwiches put up so that he would need to do no trail cooking, other than coffee, for the rest of that day, and the one to follow. Then, seeing to his canteen and to a bag of grain for the gelding, he rode out of Las Cruces, taking the road south to the forks, as he'd been directed, and there turning east.

It was at that point, when looking back upon the irregular smear of green, gray, and brown that was the settlement, that he saw the riders. There were six of them, and when he halted on a low rise to have his view of the town lying along the banks of the Rio Grande, they pulled to a stop also.

A posse. Any doubt to the contrary was dispelled when he saw the glint of sunlight on the metal stars they were wearing. He couldn't know who the men were, of course; his acquaintance with the Las Cruces law force was restricted to one man, Sheriff Eli Dirksen. But likely the remaining five in the party would be Rufe Carson, the stableman, possibly saloonkeeper Gus Underwood, and others recruited from the loafers and hangers-on who were handy.

Dirksen could have but one thing in mind. He must still be convinced that Jake was on his way to find and join his father, and by following him, he and his posse would be led to where Fritz Benedict was holed up. This accounted for the sheriff's change of attitude and his willingness to let him go his way, Jake realized.

A hard grin cracked Benedict's mouth. The hell with that! He had no idea where his father might be, but had hoped that by going to the Cornudas way station where the hijacking had taken place he could turn up some idea of where Fritz Benedict would be. That idea was out for the time; he'd not give Dirksen and his posse the satisfaction of even following him there. Instead he'd lead the lawman and his deputies off on a snipe hunt, lose them somewhere in the hills, and then continue on to Cornudas.

A sobering thought suddenly possessed Jake Benedict. In thinking about the way station he had gone right ahead and assumed that it was his father who had killed the two men and made off with the guns. The assumption had lodged in his mind just as it had in everyone else's.

Jake scrubbed vigorously at his jaw, frowned and rode on. That a man calling himself Fritz Benedict had hijacked and murdered was undeniable. Jake's contention was that it could not possibly have been his father but a stranger using his name. Was that reasonable? Fritz had written that he was heading down into that part of the territory, and aimed to settle in or around Las Cruces. There could hardly be two Fritz Benedicts with the same idea in mind.

Stirring restlessly on his saddle, and pushing the conflicting thoughts from his mind, Jake looked over his shoulder. Dirksen and his men were still coming on. Again a half grin split Jake's lips, and throwing his glance ahead, he made a swift survey of the country rolling out before him.

Towering mountains that someone had aptly named the Organs stood as a ragged, pinnacled barrier to the east. The road leading to them appeared well-traveled, and angled toward a definite gap at the northern end of the range. Beyond that point Jake was not certain what to expect—endless plains country more than likely.

The slopes sliding down from the crest were densely covered with a brittle, springy growth which he'd heard called chaparral. Mesquite was plentiful also, along with countless globular-shaped snakeweed, and sharp-pointed yucca. The main body of the mountain itself, unlike the grass and tree-covered hills of Tennessee and Missouri, looked to be of solid, forbidding rock upon which the unhampered sun beat with glistening intensity.

Jake made no effort to elude Dirksen's posse, which doggedly continued to follow his trail at a distance of a mile or so. Once he gained the pass in the rugged mountain and had dropped off onto its yonder side, he would make his move. Keeping to the center of the rutted road, now bearing southward, he pressed on, letting the bay take his own time in laboring up the grade. Coming finally to the narrow gash in the crest, Benedict halted.

Spread out before him was a vast plain. The slopes of the Organs were to his right, while to the left a fairly deep arroyo wound its way through the rocks, one filled with oak brush, chaparral and other rank growth. More mountains could be seen on the far side of the intervening bleached-looking mesa.

At once Jake swung off the road, taking a left-hand course through a maze of jumbled shale and brush. He urged the bay to as hurried a pace as he dared, being careful not to get the horse injured. After a quarter mile, with the gelding foaming with sweat and his own clothing plastered wetly to his body, Jake cut in behind a large, jutting shoulder of rock to rest and see if he had been successful in shaking the sheriff and his posse.

Minutes later Jake swore softly. The attempt had failed. He watched the lawmen break into view at the lip of the pass, and stop. For a time they remained in their saddles, and then one member of the party dismounted, and began to examine the loose dust on the shoulder of the road. Abruptly he wheeled, retraced his steps to his horse, mounted, and motioning for the others to follow, headed north into the rocks and brush. He hadn't fooled the posse at all, Benedict saw, but he had accomplished one thing; he had managed to get out of sight.

Going into the saddle at once, Jake continued along the eastern base of the Organs, taking advantage of the outcroppings of rocks, the bulging shoulders, and the thick brush. An hour or so later he reached a wide, sandy wash which veered off at right angles. It was several feet lower than the ground level he had been following. Immediately he guided the bay down into it.

The sun, a molten disc high above in an empty, clear blue sky seemed to be bearing down with greater force. Nothing appeared to be alive in the desolate area—no birds, no animals of any kind. Not even the great, broad-winged vultures that ordinarily could be spotted soaring lazily over the land were to be seen. It was no time for a man to be traveling, Benedict realized, but the stubborn need to get Eli Dirksen and his deputies off his trail refused to let him halt.

Around the middle of the afternoon the big wash played out, simply rising gradually to the level of the mesa, and disappearing. In the filigree shade of a mesquite, Jake paused to study the country behind him. His spirits lifted when he could see no signs of the lawmen, and with a heavy sigh, reckoned he'd finally lost them.

Hat off, mopping at his face and neck with his bandanna, Benedict considered his position. He was aware that he'd gone much farther north than he'd intended, but the Cornudas way station was still to the east—of that he was certain. He had only to alter course, head more into the southeast, and eventually arrive there.

Resting the bay for an hour or so in the scant shadow of the mesquite, Jake mounted and rode on. He was in broad, open country now and it disturbed him. The posse, should they be searching the mesa for him with the aid of a glass, would easily spot him as he crossed the flat, almost barren land.

But there was no help for that. He did take advantage of the occasional swales and washes, the stunted clumps of brush standing like lonely, shriveled sentinels in the breathless heat while hoping all the while that luck would be with him.

The day wore on with no letup of the heat. In an effort to ignore it Jake put his mind to other thoughts: what would he say to his father when and if he found him and they came face to face? And Letty Kellen who lived in her father's ranch somewhere in the area—what could he do to assure her that he was no criminal, no outlaw? Once Jake halted to raise himself in his stirrups and study the country ahead. Was it possible for him to bypass the Cornudas way station, lose himself in this hell of blazing sun and glittering sand?

That could not have happened, he knew. The stage stop was almost two days ride from Las Cruces, and he had not yet seen the sunset of the first. Treating himself to a small drink of tepid water from the canteen, Benedict glanced over his shoulder into the direction of the

Organs. Dirksen and his party were not in sight, but a thin haze of dust off to the south of the pass was probably them. Satisfied he had no need to worry about them, Jake corked the canteen and continued on.

He'd not reach the way station until sometime late the following day, so actually there was no chance of overshooting it. Still, it would be smart to travel in the general direction of the place. Such was not so simple.

In a strange land devoid of available significant landmarks, Jake found himself wondering if he wouldn't be as well off to double back, locate the road leading down from the pass in the Organs—an old emigrant trail, Underwood had said—follow it until it reached a place called Empty Tanks, and there turn east on what was more or less a main trail that was used by wagons heading for California years earlier. It was still well marked, and if he kept to it while maintaining an easterly course, he'd soon come to the Cornudas station.

But today was now and Jake figured he'd best think about it. He'd find a decent spot to make camp—a dry one, as finding a stream or a spring in this sprawling land of sun-blasted rock and sand was out of the question. There'd be water, he knew, in the blue-green smudge of hills lying on the horizon to both the south and the east, but they were completely beyond reach for that day and could be no part of his plans. He'd simply have to rely on the canteen, fortunately still near full, for water to satisfy the gelding and himself.

Motion just beyond a stand of head-high brush off to his right brought Benedict to a stop. Brushing at the sweat misting his eyes, he centered his attention on the edge of the growth. The head of a horse came into view. Instantly Jake spurred the bay down into a slight hollow and halted behind a sprawling clump of cholla cactus. Drawing his rifle from its boot, he slid to the ground and crouched low, waiting.

Soon, the horse was in the open, and its rider, a lean, copper-skinned man was in sight. Apaches! Benedict tensed. A second brave rode slowly out from behind the scrub brush, wearing a loosely fitting, dirty white shirt and drawers. He was followed by a third, and then a fourth until a dozen—some half-naked in the broiling sun, others clad in stained and dusty white—had made an appearance. Moving in single and double file, they followed an eastward course, one paralleling, more or less, the one Jake was taking.

Frowning, Jake watched the procession of braves move slowly away. To continue on the same line would surely bring him to the attention of the Apaches; to turn back or delay for any length of time could allow Sheriff Dirksen and his deputies to locate and resume their pursuit of him.

That gave him but one choice, Benedict decided: change course and head north into the low, rolling hills that lay in that direction. Darkness was not too far off—three or four hours, at most—and once night closed in he'd have darkness for cover. A thought came to him: could these Apaches be a part of those to whom his father had planned to sell the stolen rifles? He had noted only one or two with guns, the others carrying either bows and arrows or lances. Such was possible. If he followed them would they lead him to Fritz Benedict? That was possible, too, but how could he be sure they were the ones his father intended to deal with, or that they were headed for their village or camp, and not away from it?

Hunkered behind the cholla Jake gave the problem deep thought. Best he stick with his original plan, and go on to Cornudas, he decided. There he could get the straight of things from the station agent, Cal Hollenbeck, and get started right.

The Apaches were out of sight, having dropped beyond a low ridge into a swale of some sort. Jake turned to the bay, mounted, and cut sharply left. It wasn't too far to the low hills. He should reach them and the relative protection they would offer within a half hour or so. He'd make his camp—

A yell brought Benedict about. One of the braves had apparently pulled away from the others for some reason, and was lagging behind. He had spotted Jake immediately when the gelding had stepped clear of the cholla. The Apache was waving frantically to the rest of his party. As Benedict, startled by the Indian's unexpected appearance and piercing yell, watched in surprise, the brave suddenly bent forward on his pony and, drumming his heels into the wiry little horse's ribs, started for Jake at a dead run.

Benedict delayed no longer and, drawing his rifle from the boot, sent the bay galloping for the welter of hills. More wild yells broke the hot stillness of the mesa as the remainder of the Apaches surged up out of the swale or arroyo they were in, and joined their member in the chase. Grim, Jake jacked a cartridge into the rifle's chamber, and got set for a fight as the gelding raced on. He was lucky there were only a couple of guns in the party, otherwise his chances of reaching the hills would be considerably smaller.

He looked ahead. The broken, brushy area was not far. If he could slow the braves down a bit he could probably lose them. Raising his rifle, Jake leveled it as best he could at the oncoming riders, and triggered a shot. One of the braves flinched as the bullet passed close by—but there was no slowing down. Benedict lifted his weapon again. There was no chance to take aim, only to point the rifle in the general direction of the Apaches, and shoot. Pressing off a second shot, he swore. It had been no more effective than the first.

One of the Apaches opened up at that point. Jake forgot his rifle for the moment and crouched low as he urged the sweating bay on to faster speed across the rolling land. He heard faint, hollow cracks as the brave used his weapon. The bullets were wide, so much so that Benedict had no idea where they hit.

But the braves could get lucky, particularly if the other one that was armed began to use his gun. Jake jammed his weapon back into the boot. He'd do better to concentrate on getting away from the Indians than trying to stop them.

The bay was beginning to tire. Benedict scanned the country before him, hoping to see a suitable place where he could hole up and make a stand if necessary. A sudden break in the land would permit him to turn off, escape the eyes of the Apaches for at least a few minutes, and allow him to slacken the bay's headlong flight while he figured what was best to do.

A bluff loomed up on the right. Jake angled abruptly for it, feeling the bay tremble between his legs at the sudden change. He reached the base of the red-faced cut, rushed past it, and again turned sharp right, sending the straining bay up the somewhat steep side of the mound at a hard, labored pace. Benedict could hear the braves pouring down into the shallow valley between the hills a hundred yards or so behind him.

They could not have seen him as he doubled back up onto the bluff, and if luck was with him, the Apaches would continue straight on—at least until they realized he was no longer ahead of them. When that occurred they would circle back and begin a search for the gelding's tracks, but by then he should be well out of the area.

The bay was lagging badly. Jake, taking careful note of the land around him, swung the horse down onto a gravelly ledge that bordered a fairly deep arroyo. The hoof prints of the bay wouldn't be so easily picked up there by the braves, he reasoned, and if he could manage to stay out of sight, odds were he could get the Indians off his trail. A stand of dense brush over to the left drew his attention. Benedict hurried the weary horse toward it. Reaching the thick, tangled growth he drew to a stop, mopping at the sweat collected on his forehead and clouding his eyes. Straining, he endeavored to pick up sounds of the Apaches above the gusty wheezing of the gelding. He could hear nothing. Hopes lifted within him. Maybe his luck had held; maybe the braves had turned into the opposite direction when they came to lower ground. He could be rid of the braves.

But he would not take anything for granted. It was best not to trust in good fortune too much; it would be wise to move, to get as far from the bluff where he'd thrown off the Apaches as soon as possible. Clucking softly, he urged the bay into motion, allowing the big horse to continue through the scrubby, waist-high brush that covered the ledge, at a slow, quiet walk.

Suddenly, Jake Benedict felt himself and the bay falling. Too late he saw that the horse had come to the edge of a deep hole, one created by a second arroyo converging with the first at a right angle. Water roaring down with great force from higher levels during rainstorms in the past had made the juncture a swirling maelstrom that slashed away the earth beneath the near bank of the depression and left a wide overhang. Under the bay's weight the ground had given way.

Jake had time only to jerk his feet free of the stirrups, and throw himself backward off the saddle. An instant later his senses rocked as his head struck something with sickening force, and then blackness closed in about him.

⊷ 5 ⊷

BENEDICT stirred, then sat up slowly. He was still a bit groggy from the blow to the head he'd received, but some inner caution was prodding him relentlessly, warning him that he must rouse, get to his horse, and move on. He knew the Apaches were still nearby. Raising a hand he touched the back of his head. A stickiness there told him that he had bled considerably.

Turning over onto his knees, Jake glanced about. He was down in a sink dug into the arroyo's floor. Above him extended, like a canopy, the part of the overhang that had not given way under the weight of his horse. He had no idea how long he had lain there—only moments, he thought, but he could not be sure. Long enough, however, for the light breeze to have carried away any dust he noticed as he struggled to his feet.

The bay gelding . . . Alarm shot through Jake. He was really in trouble if the horse had broken a leg or his neck in the fall. Benedict heaved a sigh of relief. The bay was standing in the shade cast by the overhang only a few steps away. One side of the horse was plastered with sand and litter from the floor of the arroyo, but other than that he appeared to be all right.

Abruptly Jake tensed. Voices. Guttural, unfamiliar words that had no meaning to him reached his ears. The Apaches! They were on the ledge above the arroyo, evidently puzzled by his disappearance. Taut, Benedict glanced at the bay. If the horse moved even the slightest, the braves undoubtedly would hear. And if they did he was certain he'd not have time to reach the horse, mount, and make a desperate run for safety, much less get his hands on his rifle and make a successful fight of it.

The Apaches, he guessed, had tracked him to that point on the trail above the ledge, or possibly a bit beyond, and then, finding no sign of him, had turned back. Now, at a place where all traces of him had mysteriously vanished they were at a loss as to what to do next. Such was apparently the source of much disagreement and argument if the heated, angry tones of the braves' voices were any indication.

Tension clamping him in a viselike grip, Jake waited out the dragging moments, expecting with each passing breath to hear the bay shake himself, shift from one leg to another, or do something that would betray his presence. Benedict wished now he had learned to wear and use a handgun. If he had, he would not now be finding himself unarmed. But he had made a choice years earlier when a friend of his father's, a still-faced man who worked for the railroads, had advised him to never strap on a pistol unless he was sure he knew how to use one well, because the simple act of wearing one would pit him against men who did. Jake had made a decision upon receiving that bit of sage advice, and stayed with his rifle, a weapon he handled with singular expertise.

Jake became aware that the Apaches were moving off. At first he could not tell the direction they were taking as the thump of their ponies' hooves was so soft he could scarcely hear them. But soon it became apparent the Indians were turning back the way they had come, either backtracking in hope of picking up his trail again, or giving it up entirely.

The arrival of the Apaches had quickly dispelled the light-headedness brought about by the blow he'd sustained. Jake waited until he was certain the braves were gone, and then rising, crossed to the bay. Without taking time to examine the gelding, he mounted and struck off up the arroyo in the direction opposite that taken by the Apaches. After he had covered a hundred yards or so along the winding, twisting wash, he halted. Dismounting, he made a hasty check of the big horse. He could find nothing wrong, and as there had been no noticeable limp, Benedict assumed, with relief, that the bay was all right.

But he, personally, was lost. Not in the sense that he was unable to tell directions—the blue-gray mountains were far to the east, the sun, now dropping lower, was in the west—it was simply that he had worked so far north and east eluding the band of Apaches that he was uncertain now just where the Cornudas way station would be. Somewhere to the south, and a bit west, he reckoned— if he had overshot the place.

But he had best not turn southward yet. The Apaches had been headed east when he first spotted them, and he just might run into them again unless he allowed time for them to pass. Climbing back onto the bay Jake put the horse into motion with a rake of his spurs, and let him pick his way steadily along the floor of the arroyo.

The gash on his head began to smart and ache. Taking his spare bandanna, he wet it with water from the canteen and gingerly dabbed at the wound. He doubted the injury was serious, although it had bled copiously. He did experience brief waves of dizziness if he moved his head too quickly, and the rocking motion of the saddle as the bay moved on was of some aggravation.

He'd halt, make camp soon, Jake decided, glancing back at the sun. He wished he could find a creek or a spring somewhere to pull up by; he could think of few things at the moment that would feel as good as dunking his head into cold water and washing away the sweat

45

and dried blood that stiffened his skin.

He saw no more of the Apaches, which was as it should be. If they had returned to the course they had been on when he had first encountered them they would be riding due east. As near as he could determine he was veering north, or nearly so, which should take him away from the party of braves.

As for Eli Dirksen and his men, Jake had no good idea where they might be. The last he saw of them they were well to the south and west, and on his trail—more or less. When the Apaches had come into the picture, he had forgotten all about the lawmen. They really didn't matter anyway. Dirksen meant no harm, was simply tracking him in the mistaken hope that he would lead them to his father.

The question as to Fritz Benedict's guilt in the hijacking of the army guns rose again in Jake's mind. It was hard to believe that his father could involve himself in such a thing as robbery; harder still to believe that he would sell weapons and ammunition to the Indians who would in turn use them on hapless pilgrims and ranchers.

But the more Jake mulled it over, the less likely it seemed to him that Fritz was innocent of the charge. He didn't actually know his father, he realized. He guessed he would recognize him on sight, but even that was only a probability. What he didn't know was the man himself, what he was like inside. Could he be a thief, a cold-blooded killer?

Jake's shoulders stirred at the uncomfortable question. It was something he couldn't answer for the plain and simple reason that he and his father had never been close. He had known the man only in a passing way. Just what lay beneath the exterior his father displayed to his family was a mystery.

And from the way matters were shaping up Jake reckoned he never would know. Dirksen and his posse of deputies, as well as the army, were all out after Fritz, and they would no doubt kill him on sight. Jake's feeling for Fritz Benedict was neither warm nor cold; it was nothing more than neutral, and he reckoned he owed him nothing. But the man was his father, and his mother had loved him. Maybe he should try to do something about the situation. If he could find his father first, and could persuade him to forget about selling the rifles to the Apaches, leave them for the army to find, and then slip over the border into Mexico—

Jake pulled the bay up short as the sound of another horse directly ahead reached him. The Apaches again? Benedict drew his rifle. It would be a fight this time. They would have him cold, caught down in the deep arroyo as he was with only two ways to go, forward or backward—and they'd never let him do either. He was in a neat and deadly pocket. Muffling the click of the hammer as he cocked the weapon, Jake waited for the Indians to make their move.

It came almost immediately. A horse and rider appeared at a sharp bend in the wash. The man was no Apache, but was instead a lean, angular-faced cowhand.

"Whoa there, mister!" he shouted in alarm when he saw Benedict's leveled rifle. "Ain't no call for shooting!"

Relieved, Jake lowered the weapon, and laying it across his lap, smiled tightly. "Just had a run-in with a bunch of Apaches. Thought you were them coming back."

"Sure plain you been up against something," the rider said with a low whistle. "A bullet do that to your head?"

"No. Horse fell—"

"Well, whatever, it sure looks like you could do with a little fixing. Going anywhere special?"

"Cornudas way station."

Again the old cowhand whistled softly. "You're a far piece from there, friend. Mind telling me your name? Mine's Jim Canady. Friends call me Candy."

Benedict rode forward a few strides and extended his hand. "Pleased to know you, Candy. I'm Jake Benedict," he said and waited for the man's reaction—one of hostility, he was certain.

But Canady only nodded as he took Jake's hand into his own and shook it firmly. Either he was not making any connection between Jake and the hijacking of the freight wagon, or it didn't matter to him.

"You sure ain't going to make it to Cornudas today," he said with a grin. "Dang near a day's ride from here. And you ain't in no shape to be camping out. I'll just take you on to the ranch with me, and let the cook fix up your head. You can sleep in the bunkhouse with me and the rest of the crew, then take out for Cornudas in the morning."

"Sounds good to me," Jake said. "Sure don't want to put you to any trouble, however—"

"Won't be no trouble," Canady said. "You look a mite

peaked. Only rightful thing a man can do is help anoth-er'n when it's needful. Just you come along with me," he added, and wheeling his horse about, headed back up the arroyo.

"This ranch of yours," Jake said, moving up alongside the man, "it near here?"

"Five, maybe six miles," Candy replied. "And it ain't mine. Just work there. Belongs to a fellow named Tom Kellen."

## ══ 6 ══

LETTY was sitting on the front porch of the low, rambling ranch house when she saw one of the cowhands, Jim Canady, coming up the road with a stranger at his side.

It was not yet fully dark, and she was waiting supper on her father who had made a late ride down to the south part of the range where there was trouble of some sort. At first Letty thought the approaching riders were her father and one of the ranch hands, but her mistake was quickly corrected when they drew nearer, and she was afforded a better look.

The rider with Jim Canady did appear familiar; a dark, muscular man in a flat-crowned hat, colored shirt, and the usual sand-colored pants. He was forking a bay horse that looked to have had a hard day.

"Howdy, Miss Letty," Candy greeted her as he and the stranger rode into the yard. "This here fellow's Jake Benedict. Gone and got hisself hurt dodging Indians. I run across him while I was hunting strays. Aim to get

Cookie to do some doctoring—"

"No need to bother," Letty said on sudden impulse. She had recognized Benedict even as Jim Canady was announcing his name. "I'm not busy, just waiting for papa. I can take care of him."

A puzzled look pulled at Jim Canady's sharp features, and question filled his small, squinty eyes at the girl's words. But after a moment he nodded.

"Sure thing, Miss Letty. Where you want him?"

"Take him around to the back, Candy," she said. "I'll get some medicine and bandages and meet you there."

"Yes'm," Candy said, and motioning to Benedict, moved toward the rear of the house.

Letty, hurrying through the structure, paused long enough to collect what medical supplies she would need, along with a pan of hot water and a handful of clean, white rags. Benedict's head wound looked to be little more than a scratch, probably so minor that any of the crew could have taken care of it, but she had felt a stir of pleasure when she recognized Jake Benedict— and she was certain there had been interest in his pale eyes when he saw her.

He was waiting on the porch when she got there. Candy had gone on to the bunkhouse where he could clean up for supper with the rest of the crew who were not out on the range. Letty glanced at Benedict as she came through the doorway, and, setting the pan of water and the other items on a nearby table, smiled and pointed to a chair.

"Sit there—"

Benedict shrugged, and complied. To him it seemed a

lot of bother for nothing. "I don't think you need to go to all this trouble, Miss Kellen—"

"Letty," she interrupted.

"Head got hit when I went down. Probably was a rock, or maybe my horse clipped me with a hoof," he continued. "Didn't much more than break the skin."

"I'm afraid it's more than that," Letty said. "You've got a fair-sized lump there, and the cut's more than a scratch. The fall must have knocked you out."

Jake winced as Letty dabbed at the cut with a pad she had made from a bit of the rags and soaked in the hot water.

"For a bit," he admitted reluctantly. It was as if he disliked the idea of displaying any vulnerability to her, Letty thought.

"Expect you've been a bit light-headed ever since it happened . . . Candy said you got it when you ran into some Apaches. Was there any shooting?"

"No, was trying to get out of their way when my horse went over the edge of an arroyo."

Letty shook her head. "The Apaches seem to be getting all worked up over something. I guess it's that chief over in Arizona—Victorio, they call him—that's at the bottom of it. Have you turned up anything on your father yet?"

Letty noted the look of surprise that came over Jake Benedict's features. Evidently he thought she would not recall his purpose for being there, or perhaps not even remember who he was.

"Nothing yet," he said disconsolately. "Was on my way to that Cornudas way station to see what I could find out there when I ran into the Indians."

Letty, folding a strip of cloth into a second pad, saturated it with a disinfectant and applied it to the wound. Benedict recoiled from the sharp sting of the medicine coming in contact with his raw flesh, but he grinned and said nothing.

"Sorry," the girl murmured, and then began to wind a bandage about his head to hold the pad in place. "Best you wear this for a couple of days. Can't afford to let the cut mortify."

Jake got to his feet slowly and reached for his hat. "I'm sure obliged to you—"

"You're welcome . . . Now, it's best you stay here for the night. If Candy didn't mention it, you can take supper with the crew and sleep in the bunkhouse—"

Letty paused, glanced toward the hitch rack at the rear of the house. Three riders had come in and were pulling up and dismounting. Two were regular ranch hands; the third was her father.

"Here's papa," she said a bit uncertainly. "I'll have to explain—"

"Who's this?" Kellen, a high-shouldered man with a stern face, demanded as he came onto the porch. "Ain't he the son of that hijacker—Benedict?"

Letty felt her temper lift. "He's not sure of that. They just have the same name."

"Fair proof I'd say. What's he doing here on my ranch?"

"Candy brought him in. Found him on the range. He'd had a run-in with some Apaches and got hurt."

Kellen shook his head angrily. "Candy knows better

than to go bringing every saddle tramp he comes across onto my ranch. And you know better than to dirty your hands tending one."

Letty could see Jake Benedict stiffening at her father's harsh words. A hardness began to fill his eyes, and small, taut lines formed at the corners of his mouth. Abruptly a boldness came over her. Ordinarily, she was a tractable, obedient daughter, but suddenly that was at an end.

"That's not right, Papa—your saying things like that!" she declared, bright spots of anger glowing in her cheeks.

"Right or not, it's the God's truth!" Kellen thundered. "You shouldn't be talking to him—much less patching him up. Any man who'll put rifles in the hands of the Indians don't belong around decent folks—"

"I've told you, we don't know that it was his father that's doing that. Anyway, even if it is his father, Jake had nothing to do with it."

Kellen considered his daughter narrowly. "So it's Jake, is it . . . Well, there ain't no doubt in my mind that he's mixed up in it," he continued. "Same goes for the sheriff. One of the hands come across Dirksen and a posse south of here a ways. Eli's convinced he's Benedict's son, and that—"

"I'm convinced that he's not," Letty stated flatly, amazed at the belligerent stand she was taking. Never before had she defied her father outright, but now that there had been a first time, all misgivings were gone. She had done it and Tom Kellen seemed to be showing a new respect for her.

"You got anything to say about this?" the rancher said, abruptly turning to Benedict. Kellen appeared at a loss as to what he should say to his suddenly rebellious daughter.

"Only that I'm looking for the man who calls himself Fritz Benedict, to see if he's my pa or not," Jake answered.

"Ain't no doubt. Can't be—"

"I'll admit everything kind of points that way, and maybe he is my pa, but I've got to know for sure."

Kellen shook his head impatiently. "You're fooling yourself, Benedict. It's your pa all right. You just don't want to believe it—if that's the real story. Sheriff thinks you're here to join him in his dealings with the Apaches."

Benedict hung on to his temper, took a moment to look off toward the cookhouse where the cook was banging pans around as he got ready for the evening meal.

"Sheriff's wrong—"

"Expect you to say that, but that ain't neither here nor there. I ain't letting you roost here till you find out. My daughter's fixed up whatever you done to your head. Now I want you to ride out—get off Rocking K land."

"No, Papa," Letty said firmly as Jake started to turn away. "He's not going anywhere tonight. I've told him he's to eat supper with the crew, and sleep in the bunkhouse."

Kellen's face had turned a deep red as anger coursed through him. "I'll be damned if I—"

"I sure don't want to be the cause of trouble between

you two," Jake interrupted. "Best I ride on right now."

"You'll do no such a thing," Letty said firmly. "The Rocking K has never turned away a stranger in need—and it's not about to now."

"Stranger! Hell, he ain't no stranger!" Tom Kellen stormed. "He's the pup of the man who's aiming to put guns in the hands of savages who'll use them on us."

"You don't know that, Papa—you only think that's who he is. Why can't you give him the benefit of the doubt until it's proven one way or another?"

"You think we'll ever see him again after he finds his pa and they throw in together? Hell, no. He'll be long gone with his pockets full of the gold the Apaches will be paying him and his pa for them rifles they stoled."

Jake Benedict, apparently weary of the words being flung back and forth and the dissension he had caused, turned again to leave. Letty caught at his arm, halted him.

"Where are you going?"

"Best I ride on—"

"You'll do nothing of the kind!" Letty said, defiantly facing her father. "You're to stay here until morning."

Tom Kellen scrubbed at his jaw impatiently. Anger still rolled through him. It showed in the color of his face and the brightness of his eyes.

"All right then, damn it—have it your way!" he snapped. "You're a fool to go mixing in this, Letty, for taking sides with this—this drifter, but I'll let it pass. One damn thing," he added turning to Benedict, and leveling a finger at him. "You're to be gone by daylight—and if I ever catch you on my range again I'll shoot you on sight!"

## 7

B ENEDICT was up and on his way well before the deadline set by rancher Tom Kellen, not so much from fear of the hard-crusted man, but because he regretted being the source of trouble between Letty and her father, and was unwilling to further aggravate it.

He had taken supper in the mess shack with the Rocking K crew and later bedded down in the bunkhouse, seeing no more of Letty or her father. When he took his quiet leave in the early, crisp hours of the next morning, he roused Jim Canady long enough to thank him for what he had done, and asked him to convey his appreciation to the girl. The cowhand had sleepily assured Jake that he would do so.

Riding out of the Rocking K yard, Benedict struck a southeast course for the Cornudas way station, following the directions given him the night before by Candy. There'd be some low mountains also called the Cornudas, that he could use as landmarks. Point for them, Candy had advised, and he was sure to end up at the way station.

It was cool and pleasant riding along in the quiet predawn. The sky above looked dark and soft, and was filled with stars. The land rolling off flat and smooth around him was no longer gray and baked as it had been in the day, but a faintly glowing silver. The rabbit brush, gaunt cholla cactus, scraggily mesquite, and occasional rocks, so stark in the sun's punishing rays, now assumed a gentler countenance, and appeared to be made of shadows and stray shafts of starlight.

Coming as he had from a part of the country where lush grass, large trees, and sparkling streams were common and taken for granted, he had wondered when he first saw the vast emptiness of the new territory how anyone could choose to make a home in this land of barren ruggedness.

But there was a singular beauty to it all, Jake had finally come to admit. The endless plains, the rolling hills, the arching, clean blue sky with its occasional billows of cottony clouds, the gray-blue mountains reaching up to pierce the heavens, the few creeks and rivers with their cargos of precious water—it all made for a different world from the one he had grown up in.

Yet, in so short a time Jake Benedict had become drawn to it—to the bright, clean days, the continual, hot sunshine, to even the wind that rose now and then to snatch up particles of glistening sand and sweep them up in boiling, restless clouds.

It would be a fine place to live, Jake found himself agreeing. He could see why men like Tom Kellen were so fiercely possessive of what they owned. He'd like to think that his father had grown to like the country and had chosen it as a new home for his family—but such was hardly possible. Fritz Benedict had made the long journey down into New Mexico territory all right, perhaps with the idea in mind to start a horse ranch. But something had gone wrong; something that caused him to change, to become an outlaw instead.

Jake, staring out across the luminescent flats to a line of reddish bluffs, shook his head. It seemed impossible that such could have taken place—that Fritz Benedict, admittedly not the most constant and devoted of fathers, but honest and trustworthy nevertheless—would forsake such values and turn outlaw.

Smoke . . . Jake halted the bay near a clump of mesquite and considered the thin, dark plume twisting up into the steadily brightening sky. A camp of some sort, he reckoned—and most likely Apache. Accordingly, cutting hard to the right, Benedict began to circle the area.

Keeping to low ground when available, and taking advantage of each clump of sparse growth, Jake continued on his way. He could see the Cornudas Mountains now, a low, dark mass lying on the southern horizon. They looked much nearer than they actually were. He had learned earlier that in the high, clear atmosphere of the southwest apparent distance was deceiving.

Voices brought Benedict to a stop again. At that moment, in a low swale between two mounds, he glanced about for cover and saw there was none of consequence. He could only hope the saddle he was crossing was enough below the general level of the plain to prevent his being seen.

Luck was with him. The heads of three braves appeared briefly above the roll of land beyond the depression, and quickly disappeared. Evidently they were moving toward the camp he had skirted. Waiting out a long quarter hour to be certain the braves he had seen were gone and that there were no more in the immediate area, Jake rode on. He continued to keep well to the west of the smooth hills where the Apaches had made their camp, but bearing always for the Cornudas Mountains.

The day wore on, the heat intensifying with the passage of each hour. Finally he halted in a brushy coulee where there had once flowed a spring, to rest and squeeze a little water from a wet rag into the mouth of the gelding. He took the time also to eat a bite of lunch. He'd not bothered to stop for breakfast. The supper he'd enjoyed at Kellen's Rocking K had been a big one, and he'd felt no hunger until then—midafternoon.

He would have appreciated a cup of coffee, but it would be foolhardy to risk a fire with Apaches in the vicinity. Too, he had only the water in his canteen, now less than half full, for the bay and himself. With his lack of knowledge of the country, and the apparent drought that was holding sway, he considered it only prudent to conserve his supply as much as possible.

Late in the day, with the dark blue mountains lying to the south now a reality, Benedict again saw smoke. It appeared to rise from somewhere a few miles east of the ragged formations. Cornudas no doubt, he decided, and urged the weary bay into a slow lope.

There wasn't much to the way station, Jake saw an hour or so later, as he rode up to the cluster of low, adobe-and-wood structures. A main building, a fairly large pole corral fronting a stable, two or three small sheds, and a water well made up the Cornudas stagecoach stop.

A tall, angular man in bib overalls, stovepipe boots, and a dusty, peaked hat atop a shock of thick white hair was in the fenced area working on the leg of a horse. Beyond him a second man—Mexican or Indian, Jake could not be sure which—was raking in front of the stable.

"Howdy! Step down if you're of a mind," the man attending the horse invited Jake as he straightened up. A smile cracked the man's leathery features and, brushing at his trailing handlebar mustache, he added, "I'm Cal Hollenbeck. I look after things around here."

"Name's Benedict," Jake said. Leaving the saddle and moving up the gate, he opened it and entered.

Hollenbeck, hand extended in welcome, frowned. "You say Benedict?"

"Yeah, Jake Benedict."

The station agent lowered his arm. "You any kin to a man called Fritz Benedict?"

Jake shrugged. "Why I'm here. Aim to find out if I am."

Hollenbeck spat. "Hell, a man ought to know who's kin and who ain't."

"Expect that's so. I've been over in Las Cruces hunting my pa. Heard about the hijacking. Didn't sound like my pa would be the one who did it. Rode over here to see what I could find out."

"His name Fritz?"

"Yes—"

"Can't see why you're pussyfooting around about it for then! Was Fritz Benedict that hijacked them rifles, and killed two men. I know 'cause he hung around here for a couple of days before he done it. Besides that, one of the fellows he shot down named him before he died."

Jake glanced off toward the stable. The man there had obtained a wheelbarrow and was now loading it with the trash he'd raked into a pile.

"I look anything like the Fritz Benedict you're talking about?"

Hollenbeck scratched thoughtfully at the stubble of beard on his chin. "Now, I can't say yes and I sure can't say no. Was a mite on the heavy side, dark, was wearing a beard and mustache. That sound anything like your pa?"

Jake shook his head. "Haven't seen him in years so I don't know exactly what he'd look like. Reckon I'll recognize him if we ever come face to face."

"Yeah, expect you will." The old station agent's attitude had softened somewhat as if he now understood Jake's problem. "I take it you're maybe a bit feared that the man that took them rifles and done the killings is your pa."

Hollenbeck had seen through him quickly, Benedict realized. "Just want to be sure one way or the other," he said.

The station agent leaned up against the fence, removed his hat and brushed at the sweat on his forehead. "Said you hadn't seen him in years. You know for certain he's around here?"

Jake explained how the last word he and his mother had received from Fritz told them he was going down into the Las Cruces country of New Mexico territory to start a horse ranch, and that they'd heard no more from him since then.

Hollenbeck considered that as he glanced toward the main building of the way stop. "Your ma around here somewhere, too?"

"No, she died. Was no reason for me to stay on the farm back in Tennessee after that, so I sold out and headed this way to find pa and throw in with him."

Hollenbeck was silent for a long minute, then said, "Well, could be there's two Fritz Benedicts, but I'm mighty doubtful. Best you sort of set yourself for the truth. You ain't seen your pa for years, and a man could sure change in that much time. Things happen to him— hard luck for one thing, or maybe he takes up with another woman that sets him to thinking wrong and turns him square around from what he was aiming to do."

"Can't argue with that, but I'm finding it hard to believe that pa could become an outlaw."

"Sure wouldn't be the first time a good man went wrong. It's the easy way out of hard times, if you want to know the fact," Hollenbeck said, stepping back and untying the rope holding the horse he was working on to the top bar of the corral.

"Thing for you to remember is that you oughtn't be judging him until you know the whole story. You don't know what he might've gone through during the time he wasn't around. I'll say this—it must've been something mighty bad to've turned him into a killer and a thief."

Jake flinched involuntarily at the terms. All that Cal Hollenbeck said was true, he had to admit that. He really didn't know his father, or what his life might have been like after he forsook Tennessee. Things could happen to a good man that would change his outlook and his values and turn him into a stranger. Such could have occurred to Fritz.

"Can you put me up here for a few days?" Jake asked as Hollenbeck slapped the horse on the rump and sent him trotting for the stable.

"Sure. Got a couple of extra bunks in the station. You're plenty welcome to one, but I ain't so certain you'll have much luck finding your pa. The army's got a patrol out combing the country, same as Eli Dirksen, the sheriff at Las Cruces has—"

"I know. Had a talk with him."

"He's had posses out looking everywhere, too. Ain't nobody turned up nothing."

"Kind of hard to see how he could hide so good around here," Jake said, glancing out over the flats. "Where could he find a place where a wagon wouldn't be seen?"

Hollenbeck, ushering Jake through the gate, and pulling it closed behind him, shrugged. "Might surprise you, but it'd be danged easy. Lots of brushy draws and canyons where a fellow could go. And then there's the mountains—the Cornudas south of here, and the Guadalupes on to the east. Benedict's probably holed up somewhere in them right now, if he ain't already made a deal with the Apaches . . . You want to stable your horse? Forgot to ask."

"Be obliged to you," Jake said as they walked slowly toward the main building. "When you got time I'd like to talk to you about the hijacking."

"Sure thing," the station agent said. Then looking over his shoulder, he shouted, "Jose, come get this here horse and take care of him . . . Probably ain't much I can tell you about that that you ain't already heard if you've been talking to Dirksen," Hollenbeck continued as they resumed the short walk to the station. "Benedict hung around here a bit, like I said—resting his horse he claimed. I reckon he knew the freight wagon was due, and he was just killing time till it got here.

"Well, it did. A driver and a shotgun, and a six-man escort—civilians. The army was supposed to be here to meet the wagon and take over, and escort it on to Fort Bliss. They never showed up. Found out later that some pilgrim passing through had brought word to the soldiers that the wagon would be four or five hours late, so they just took their time coming."

"You figure it was the hijacker that sent word? Don't see how he could have ridden to them and then—"

"Expect he sent it, that he talked to somebody going through to carry the word. Anyway, things getting hung up like they was, Austin, he was the teamster, got anxious and drove on without the soldiers."

"Couldn't the civilian escort that rode in with the wagon finish the job?"

"Nope. Fellow leading it said they'd been paid to go this far, and that's what they'd done. Turned right around and headed back for wherever they'd come from soon as they'd watered their horses. I recollect Henry Austin laughing about it when I told him he best wait for the army. Said with that shipment of guns and cartridges he was hauling, him and Nate Willoughby, the shotgun, could hold off the whole Apache nation if they had to.

"Well, it wasn't the Indians that got them. This Benedict was waiting for them down the road a piece. Guess Henry and Nate wasn't expecting no trouble from him because he just up and shot them off the wagon seat, and they didn't even draw a gun.

"I heard the shooting, and went hightailing it down there. Found them both laying off in the weeds, and the team and wagon gone. Henry was dead but Nate was still living. Told me what happened. Said it was this fellow Benedict that done it, that he'd rode right out after they had arrived—he'd seen him—so he knew what he was talking about. Nate died telling me about it. I went to the station then, got the team and the buckboard, and hauled Henry and him back here. Buried them out behind the stable."

Hollenbeck halted, swiped at the sweat on his face. "I reckon that's all there is to it. The army showed up a hour or two after the shooting, and started right into hunting Benedict, but it was near dark and they soon had to give it up."

They had reached the front of the way station and were about to enter when Hollenbeck halted, his glance fixed on a cloud of dust off to the east.

"Expect that'll be them soldier boys coming back from doing their hunting. Got a young lieutenant by the name of Forrest leading them . . . Let's just hold up here for a minute. Could be they've had some luck this time and collared Benedict."

## 8

BUT LIEUTENANT FORREST and his special patrol of a dozen or so troopers had failed again. Dusty, sweaty, their faces haggard from hours of fruitless riding, the soldiers pulled up to the hitch rack and halted. Then, when the order was given, and with much squeaking of leather, all dismounted and all but Forrest headed for the pump and water trough at the corner of the building.

Forrest himself, stiff, militarily formal, wiped his youthful face with a yellow neckerchief, and crossed to where Jake and Cal Hollenbeck stood watching. The officer nodded crisply to the station agent.

"Any word from Dirksen?"

Hollenbeck shook his head. "Nope. Fact is there ain't nobody been by . . . Can see you didn't have no luck."

Forrest's mouth was set tight. "Covered every foot of ground between here and the Guadalupes, turned up nothing. Did run into one of the sheriff's posses. Said a fellow had showed up in Las Cruces claiming to be Benedict's son. It set me to wondering—"

"This is him right here, Lieutenant," Hollenbeck cut in, nodding at Jake. "Come here to look for his pa."

Forrest, sharp-faced, around thirty or so, with dark hair, brown eyes, and wearing his authority like a suit of armor, shifted his attention to Jake.

"So you're Benedict's son," he said in an accusing tone.

"Maybe," Jake replied coldly. Forrest's surly attitude

66

angered him.

"Now, what the hell's that mean? Either you are or you aren't."

"Jake here thinks this jasper that hijacked the freight wagon ain't his pa, but somebody else using the name—"

"Not likely," the officer said bluntly, brushing aside the explanation. "I expect the truth is that you're here to join him—that maybe you're the link between Benedict and the Apaches."

"Think what you damn please," Jake snapped, "but you're dead wrong."

Forrest smiled coolly, and glanced to the trough where the cavalrymen were watering their horses.

"Be damn careful how much you let those horses drink, Sergeant!" he called. "I don't want any of them foundering."

A squat, beefy soldier with the chevrons of a buck sergeant on his sleeve glanced up and nodded wearily to the officer.

"We ain't about to, Lieutenant," he said in a patient voice. "No, sir, we ain't about to."

"Just where were you expecting to meet your father?" Forrest asked, abruptly turning to Jake. The tone of the question was such that it left no doubt an answer was to be given.

Jake smiled dryly at the officer. "Figured you might tell me that. I'm a stranger around here."

Forrest swore, his eyes bright with anger. "Hell, you can't make me believe you're not here to meet that outlaw! Sheriff's of the same opinion."

"You're both wrong. If I knew where the man who's calling himself Fritz Benedict was, I'd be there now—not here wasting time bandying words with you."

The officer studied Benedict with half-closed, appraising eyes. "Something tells me you're a goddamn liar—"

Benedict's temper flared like gunpowder touched by a match flame. His balled fist lashed out, caught Forrest on the point of his chin. The officer's face filled with surprise, he staggered back and sat down hard on the loose dust and sand. Hollenbeck caught Benedict by the shoulders, restraining him further, while the soldiers at the trough looked on with indifference, and did nothing more.

After a few moments, Forrest got to his feet slowly, features red, eyes sparking. Hollenbeck, hiding his amusement, released his grip on Jake, and shook his head.

"You sure did ask for that, Lieutenant."

Forrest seemed about to reply, but thought better of it. Reaching down he picked up his campaign hat, dusted it off against a knee, and returned it to its proper place on his head.

"As an officer of the United States Army in charge of this investigation, I want to know what your plans are," he said, folding his arms across his chest and facing Jake. "A crime has been committed against the government, and frankly, I think you're in on it."

"Best you back off that idea, Forrest," Benedict said quietly.

"No, I'm after the truth," the officer declared, "and I'll

keep after it till I get it. I've got to think about all the people in this part of the country who'll suffer, even die at the hands of the Apaches because of this Fritz Benedict and his greed—and I'm still saying you've a hand in it."

Anger again rushing through him, Jake Benedict, fists knotted at his sides, took a step toward the officer. Cal Hollenbeck's big hands once again caught him by the shoulders.

"Ain't no need for that, son," the station agent said. "I reckon the lieutenant's just trying to do his job."

"He'll get no help from me—not now," Benedict said.

"What I would expect," Forrest countered. "And your attitude more or less proves what I think—that you're here to join up with that outlaw."

Abruptly, the officer spun on a heel and marched stiffly over to where his men waited. "Mount up, Sergeant. We'll bivouac over there below the stable again."

At once the troopers moved to their horses, and on command, swung up into the saddle. They waited until Forrest was set and had moved out to lead, and then followed the officer out of the yard.

Jake watched them move off. When they had rounded the corner of the corral and were disappearing behind the stable, he turned to Hollenbeck.

"That where they usually camp?"

The way station man pointed off across the low hills. "Nope. There's a spring about five miles south of here," he said, a puzzled frown on his features. "First time he ain't gone there. Seemed to always figure my place was off limits to his yellowlegs. Ain't sure what's changed his thinking."

"I am," Jake said, smiling. "He wants to keep an eye on me."

Hollenbeck nodded vigorously. "By hell—that's it! He's got it fixed in his head that this Fritz Benedict is your pa and you're aiming to meet him."

"He's partly right, I reckon," Jake said. "I'll be obliged for the use of that bunk you mentioned, and for taking care of my horse. Want to pay for both."

Hollenbeck moved past Jake to the front of the way station. Opening the dust-clogged screen door, he motioned for Benedict to enter.

"Ain't no charge—not for none of it," he said, smiling broadly. "Seeing the look on that lieutenant's face when you knocked him on his ass was worth a'plenty! He's been needing a taking-down. Seemed to think that them lieutenant's bars and that uniform made him God Almighty Himself . . . You ain't eat yet, I expect."

"No—"

"Fine. I'll scrape something together and have it ready in a few minutes. Room right through that door," Hollenbeck added, pointing, "is where you'll find your bunk. I'll have Jose bring in your gear—"

"Leave it where it is," Jake said. "There's nothing I'll be needing." He glanced about the station. The place was like a small general store with canned goods, boxed biscuits, tobacco, and a limited stock of liquor as well as a few personal items on shelves at one end of the room. Otherwise it was occupied by a large, circular, revolving center table surrounded by a number of straight-backed chairs, a long couch over which a tanned cowhide had been thrown, and a lesser table upon which were several yellowing magazines and newspapers.

"This ain't a relay station no more, but folks get stranded here now and then for a day or two—sick or maybe just plain tired of traveling," Hollenbeck said, noting Jake's interest. "Try to make it as easy and comfortable as I can for them. Lord knows this ain't the kindest country in the world to go traipsing across.

"Now, if you're not of a mind to stretch out and do some resting, you can come on into the kitchen with me and we can talk. That's something I don't seem to ever get enough of nowadays—talking with the right kind of people . . . There ought to be some warm coffee on the stove."

"Sounds good to me," Benedict said, and followed the older man across the room to a curtained doorway in the rear wall.

Thrusting aside the drapery, the agent led the way into an area with walls of shelving, a worktable, several chairs, and a large cook stove.

"Ain't got much use for all this now that we ain't a regular meal stop," Hollenbeck said, gesturing at the huge stove. "Cooking for me and Jose Chavez, and maybe a pilgrim like yourself now and then is about all I have to do nowadays." The station man paused, then pointed at the table. "Set yourself down while I pour you out a cup of coffee. I expect it's hot enough," he added, laying his hand on the side of the smoke-stained granite pot.

"It'll be fine no matter what," Jake said, settling onto

one of the chairs. "Had to pass up boiling me some java on my way here. Indians."

Hollenbeck, in the act of filling two tin cups with simmering brew paused and looked around. "They jump you?"

Jake shook his head. "Was able to dodge them. I run into them in those choppy hills north of here."

Cal swore. "Dang critters! They're just spoiling for trouble—all on account of Victorio and old Cobre. I'm sure hoping they don't get their hands on them rifles and all that ammunition. Be hell to pay for certain. Was any of the bunch carrying guns?"

"Saw only a couple or three," Jake replied as Hollenbeck set the filled cups on the table.

"Probably a hunting party from Cobre's *rancheria*. He's the chief of the plains tribes—the mountain tribes ain't been stirring around much, leastwise not yet. You know if Cobre was one of them?"

"Sure don't. Never laid eyes on him in my life. Fact is all Apaches look alike to me. Could tell who was who in the ones back home, but out here it's different."

"Where's home?" the station man asked, taking a swallow of coffee and then rising to cross to the stove.

"Tennessee—the Cumberland Gap country."

Hollenbeck removed one of the round stove lids, and taking two or three pieces of kindling from the box nearby, shoved them into the firebox.

"Ain't never been there," he said. "Always heard it was mighty pretty country. I'm from up Nebraska way myself. Beans and bacon fat suit you? Ain't got much else to offer without doing a lot of fixing. Can open us a

72

can of peaches."

"Be fine," Benedict said again, and looked around as the heavy curtain was pulled aside and the man he'd seen working in the corral entered. Hollenbeck, setting a kettle on the stove, waved a hand at him.

"This here's Jose Chavez. Helps me around the station," he said, and then to the swarthy, dark-eyed man added, "Shake hands with Jake Benedict, Jose. He's here looking for his pa."

Chavez, his features suddenly stilled, accepted Benedict's hand with obvious reluctance. *"Bienvenido, senor,"* he murmured.

"He ain't sure whether the Benedict everybody's looking for around here is his pa," Cal Hollenbeck explained, noting the withdrawn attitude of the Mexican. "He's come here to find out for sure."

A half smile parted Chavez' lips. *"Comprendo,"* he said, and turning, started back for the curtained doorway. "I have more work to do—"

"Supper'll be ready in a little while," the station man called after the departing man, and then, adding a bit of water to the kettle, nodded to Jake. "What Chavez said when he was leaving was that he savvied—understood. I reckon you don't know any Mex."

"No, sure don't," Benedict said, finishing off the last of the coffee in his cup. Hollenbeck had now turned to slicing off chunks of bacon into the pot of beans. "Aim to learn, however, if I stay down here . . . Want to ask you about the Apaches."

"Shoot," the agent said. The captivating odor of boiling beans and bacon was beginning to fill the room now. "Sure answer what I can."

"Where'll I find the main Apache village—the one where this chief Cobre will be?"

"Ain't called a village, it's called a *rancheria*. You ain't aiming to go there are you?"

Jake shrugged. "If this Fritz Benedict is figuring to sell them guns, then that's the place I'll probably find him, because he'll show up there sooner or later."

"Yeah, reckon that makes sense—unless he's already gone and made hisself a deal and handed over the rifles."

"Have to gamble on that. But I kind of doubt it. Like I said the ones I saw yesterday were carrying bows and arrows and lances, mostly. Were only two or three with rifles. Could mean pa—this Fritz Benedict—hasn't turned them over to them yet."

"Adds up, but I ain't so sure your going right to old Cobre's *rancheria* like you're figuring to do is smart. You don't know their lingo, and with them just itching to go on the warpath—"

"If I see a white man with a team and wagon, I reckon I'll know all I need to. Can do what I have to then."

Hollenbeck, stirring the kettle, wagged his head.

"I don't know but I guess it's like somebody once said—sometimes a man ain't got enough sense to be scared. Fits you, I expect."

Jake laughed. "Reckon it could, but I can't think of any better way to go at it. Army and the sheriff's posses ain't doing any good. Maybe they haven't tried watching the Apache *rancheria* like I'm aiming to do."

"Like as not. Forrest'd stay clear of them because of

the treaties. Dirksen would, too. When you figure to go?"

"Midnight. Want to be sure Forrest ain't around to see me leave."

Hollenbeck nodded. "That's a smart idea. You for damn sure don't want him dogging your trail. One man maybe'll be able to get into old Cobre's wickiups—a bunch of soldiers sure wouldn't, even if they wanted."

"That's how I see it. And I'll be obliged to you if you don't tell the lieutenant where I've gone."

"Can bank on that," Hollenbeck said with a grin. "There's a lot of soldier boys I cotton to, but I just don't take to Forrest . . . Grab yourself a plate and some eating tools off the shelf and dive in. Grub's ready."

⊷ 9 ⊷

"HEAD NORTHEAST when you ride out," Cal Hollenbeck said as Jake led his horse, now fed and rested, from the stable. It was past midnight and the stars and a strong moon were flooding the land with soft, glowing light.

"How far to the Apache camp?" Benedict asked, halting to let the station agent open the corral gate.

"Twenty mile or so—you won't miss it. Old Cobre picked hisself a place in a grove of trees that sticks out like a finger from the mountain. Creek there, too. Now, that's where he was last time I heard. Could've moved on by now. Apaches are kind of footloose. Don't stay put in one place for long. Usually just pick up and leave when firewood gets scarce, and the hunting gets poorly . . . When you aim to come back?"

"Hard to say," Jake replied, going up into the saddle. "I figure to just hang around the Apaches for a bit, and watch for my pa to show up with the guns."

"If he ain't already done that," Hollenbeck said. "Been a few days since the hijacking."

"Don't think it'll take long to find out if that's the way of it. The braves'll be carrying new rifles and making a big show of them, I expect."

"You're right there. Something bothering me about all this, though. You're talking like all you've got to do is find Cobre's *rancheria,* and then stand around and wait. It ain't that easy. You sure can't let any of them redskins see you hanging around, much less let them catch you. The way things are around here now between the Apaches and the white folks—you could turn up dead."

"Don't fret none about that. I'm in no hurry to get buried out here on the flats somewhere . . . Don't Forrest know where Cobre's camp is?"

"Sure. Expect just about everybody around here does—"

"Can figure on the army having been there then—"

"Not close. Like I said, Forrest and Dirksen maybe've rode by, but that'd be about all. It just don't pay to go poking around Apache wickiups! Anyway, the army's got orders to leave them alone unless they catch them red-handed doing something bad . . . I still ain't sure this is such a good idea."

"Could be you're right, but what else can I do? Nothing gained just hanging around here—Pa sure won't be coming back. Only thing I can see to do is get out and track him down. Maybe I can get lucky, find him before he's done any trading with the Indians—and talk him out of it."

"Well, that's a right good plan," Hollenbeck said, looking off into the pale distance beyond the corral where a coyote had begun to voice his discordant laments. "But I've got some powerful misgivings. A greenhorn like you—now I don't mean nothing bad when I call you that—waltzing right up to old Cobre's *rancheria* to hang around like you aim to do is easy to say, only it ain't going to be like that. Some of them braves or squaws are bound to spot you, and—"

"Did quite a bit of hunting back home," Jake said. "Can make my way about in the brush quiet as any Indian I ever knew . . . You said the village was in a grove of trees. Won't be hard then to work my way in from the back or the side, get close, and find a place to hide and wait."

Hollenbeck, still doubtful, rubbed at his whiskery jaw. "Well, maybe. If a man was right careful, I expect he could keep from getting caught. But he'd sure need a powerful lot of luck."

"Can use all of that I can get, but I learned a long time ago not to depend on it . . . Obliged to you for all the favors. I'll drop back and let you know how things turned out."

"Just you do that," the station agent said as Benedict pulled away. "Good luck, or *buena suerte* as they say in Mex."

"Thanks, and the same to you," Jake responded.

Taking his bearings from the way station, the pole star,

and the distant, dim, and ragged horizon that was the Sacramento Mountains, Benedict put the gelding to a good lope and rode out. He would like to get off the level prairie, and reach cover of some sort before daylight if he could. But unfamiliar with the country as he was, Jake realized he had no choice but to strike out and hope for the best. The land itself, although mostly devoid of large growth, did offer many arroyos and washes, as well as low hills that did provide some degree of concealment.

But it would be much better and considerably safer if he could gain the grove of trees in which Cobre and his people had established their camp. He needed a look at the *rancheria* and its location before deciding just what he could do. If he was fortunate enough to find the Apaches at one end of the grove, he could enter at its opposite end and work his way through to the camp. He would not know if that was possible until he got there, however.

Jake was hopeful that his plan would work. As he had told Cal Hollenbeck, he could think of no other way to get in touch with his father. Fritz Benedict could be anywhere, hiding in some remote section of the hills or plains with the wagon load of guns, waiting for things to quiet down before venturing out to strike a deal with the Apaches. And preventing Fritz from doing just that was the only hope Jake had of keeping his father from further outlawry.

His father . . . The battle that had been raging within Jake Benedict's conscience had somewhere along the line tipped to favor Sheriff Eli Dirksen, Lieutenant Forrest, and all the others who were certain that the Fritz Benedict who had committed the hijacking was no other than his father. At first, Jake had stubbornly refused to believe such could be the truth, but logic had finally won out and the bitter battle between parental loyalty and the apparent facts came to an end. He felt he could do nothing but accept what was inevitable.

Near daylight Benedict drew to a halt in a shallow draw. Two riders were moving toward him from the east—cowhands he saw with relief and not Apaches. Likely they were men who worked for Tom Kellen. Waiting until they were directly opposite, Jake then rode out of the draw. Both men, startled by his sudden and unexpected appearance, drew their pistols and wheeled their horses about sharply.

"Damn it to hell—don't be doing that!" one of the pair shouted angrily when he recognized Benedict. "Way things are with the Apaches around here right now, it's lucky we didn't blow your head off!"

The second rider, holstering his weapon, pulled off his hat and ran fingers through his hair. "Ain't you the fellow Candy brought in to the ranch the other day for fixing up?"

"Reckon I am," Jake answered. "Sure didn't mean to scare you. Where you headed?"

"Back to the ranch. Been over to the Seven Rivers country looking at some cattle. Tom figured maybe there was some rustled stock in the bunch. Wasn't. Where you going?"

"Looking for Cobre's village."

Both stared at Benedict in amazement. The older man

found his voice. "For hell's sake why? You looney?"

"Figured that would be the best place to find my pa."

The younger cowboy, rolling himself a cigarette, nodded. "Yeah, probably right, him being the one that's aiming to sell all them guns to the Apaches."

"Hoping to stop him from doing that, if I can. Or if I ain't too late," Jake said, and passing the time of day with the pair, rode on.

Around midmorning he saw smoke trickling upward into the sky well to his left, and pausing again to get his bearings, concluded the dark plume could only be rising from the Apache village. Accordingly, he began to veer more to the east, traveling steadily toward the now more definite Guadalupes. An hour or so after spotting the smoke, he reached the first outcropping of rocks and brush marking the base of the mountains. He was still off to the south of the *rancheria,* however—which was what he had planned on—and guiding the bay into the brush where he was not likely to be noticed by anyone, Jake began to work his way north through the grove.

He heard sounds coming from the Apache village long before catching sight of it: the shrill voices of children at play, men calling back and forth, a lone gunshot, the dull thud of rocks being pounded together as someone went about a chore—probably that of grinding corn, Benedict guessed.

Jake walked ahead of his horse for the last quarter mile, keeping deep in the brush until he reached a point in the dense growth that offered cover for both him and the gelding. Only a part of the camp was visible to him from that position. He could see a number of lodges—"wickiups" Hollenbeck had called them—all circular arrangements of several saplings bent and lashed together to form a dome, and then covered with what looked to Jake like a little of everything—hides, bits of canvas, cloth, blankets, even brush.

Several horses were in a makeshift corral at the edge of the camp, and although there was but one fire going at the moment, several blackened areas marked spots where others had been.

None of the Apaches were visible from where he was standing. Picketing the bay securely and taking his rifle, Benedict made his way carefully forward until he had a complete view of the camp. It was much larger than he had anticipated and there was a fairly large number of Apaches around, several of whom were gathered in a circle in front of a wickiup placed more or less in dead center of the *rancheria*. The lodge of Cobre, the chief, no doubt.

Women were moving about in the hot sunshine, some gathering wood from a supply that had been dragged in from the grove, others working at softening skins, pounding corn into meal, sewing, or doing other duties expected of their sex. Two dozen or more children romped about, most of them on a grassy berm that bordered the creek Cal Hollenbeck had mentioned. There were few dogs to be seen, lean, emaciated animals that showed little inclination to stir themselves unless driven to move by sharp words or a kick from a passing brave or squaw.

There was no sign of the wagon or of a white man.

Jake realized that could mean much, or little; but since he saw no evidence of new rifles among the braves, his spirits lifted. Fritz Benedict had not yet arrived with the stolen guns, and if Cobre and his clan were the intended purchasers, he was in time, and had only to wait.

Which was much easier to speak of than do. He would need to be on the alert every moment he was there, and on the lookout for any brave or squaw, or even a child who might for some reason wander into the brushy section where he was hiding.

It meant continual vigilance, for if he saw any of the tribe heading his way, he would need time to move quickly before the Apache was near enough to catch sight of him. The bay would be the big problem if such occurred, and whether to risk leaving the horse in the pocket in the brush or chance leading him away would be something he'd have to decide when the circumstances presented themselves.

The fact that he was there so close to Cobre's camp would stand in his favor, he felt. The Apaches would never expect anyone other than a member of the clan to risk being that near, and so would not become suspicious. It seemed to Jake that only a bad break could get him in trouble.

The day wore on, hot and dry. Braves came and went, some in breechclouts and knee-high horsehide moccasins, others wearing loose white drawers and shirts, and all with a band of cloth about their heads. Women dressed in full, ankle-length skirts, baggy blouses, and low moccasins, their black hair pulled into a thick knot at the back of the head and secured with a bit of rag, went stolidly about their tasks, some with babies bound to cradle boards slung from their shoulders.

When it became cooler, activity would pick up, Jake reckoned, and with the same thought hoped that his father with the hijacked rifles would put in an appearance—if that was to be the way of it. But waiting under such conditions, with the ever-present danger of being discovered hanging over him like a threatening cloud, kept Jake Benedict filled with tension.

Finally, the sun sank behind the horizon to the west. Gradually, the Apache *rancheria* came to life. More women appeared on the bleak compound. Several began to build fires in front of the family wickiup, after which they set about preparing the evening meal. Large pots, apparently containing a stew mix of some sort, were hung from wooden tripods over the flames by some, while others simply placed the blackened iron vessel on the half circle of rocks within which the fire had been built. Still others, preferring a different menu, set about roasting skewered chunks of meat over the smoky flames.

The braves forsook their leisure and began to stir, wandering from one wickiup to another, laughing and shouting back and forth, visiting the creek for a cooling drink of water, or making brief trips into the brush that all but encircled the camp. Even the dogs, summoning energy, got to their feet and started moving aimlessly about, sniffing and scratching.

It was risky to remain where he was any longer, Jake

realized. At any moment one of the Apaches could take it in mind to venture into the area where he was hiding. Giving it no further consideration, Benedict dropped back to where he had picketed the bay and, taking up the reins, headed for the lower end of the grove with the horse.

He froze. Motion in the brush ahead stalled him in his tracks and filled him with tension. Taut, he glanced hurriedly about seeking a better place from which to make a stand. He knew he could not risk using his rifle except as a club; a gunshot would bring the whole village down on him.

A thick clump of brush was the answer, but only partly so. It could hide him but not the bay gelding. He'd have to risk the horse being noticed; in that the odds were all in his favor as the animal was a dark brown and blended well in the shadows and failing light.

Leaving the gelding where he stood, and moving quietly, Jake stepped behind the largest clump of close-by brush. Rifle ready, he waited. Likely, it was one of the braves returning from a hunt, although he seemed to recall that Indians ordinarily went out in parties for such purpose.

The quiet thud of the oncoming horse's hooves and the soft swish of a leafy branch reached Benedict. The Apache was almost abreast the stand of thimbleberry. Jake raised his rifle, preparing to bring it down on the man's head. He caught himself, swore softly, and lowered the weapon. The startled face staring at him through the half dark was that of Letty Kellen.

## 10

"WHAT THE HELL—" Benedict muttered, stepping back.

Letty, her own rifle coming up quickly, checked abruptly. "I—I thought you were an Apache," she said.

Throwing a glance about to make certain they were alone, Jake grinned wryly. "Same here. Sure glad it wasn't any darker. I was all primed to club whoever it was . . . Let's get away from the camp."

Taking the reins of the bay, and with Letty Kellen close behind, Jake led the way back through the grove. He halted at a point where he could still have a fair view of the *rancheria* but was relatively safe from prying eyes, then secured the horses and turned to the girl.

"I want to know what you're doing here," he demanded, his voice betraying his annoyance.

"I came looking for you," Letty stated flatly. "Of all the fool things to do, coming here is—"

"Only way I can get in touch with Pa is to hang around the Apaches until I see him coming, then head him off so's I can do some talking—"

"What did you think the Apaches would be doing all that time? Once they see that wagonload of rifles, they'll go crazy. Nobody—nothing—will be able to stop them from taking over."

"I know that. It's a chance I'll have to take . . . How'd you know I'd be here?"

"One of the cowboys. He and another of the crew ran

into you this morning. You told them where you were headed. They couldn't believe it—figured you'd gone looney or something—so they watched you. Sure enough, you turned north after you got into the grove."

"Can't see as it was any business of theirs—"

"Probably would've been the way they looked at it, only they remembered you coming to the ranch and figured I ought to know what you were doing. Wasn't hard to find you. I just rode to the grove and turned north, too."

"I still don't understand why—"

Letty, her face a pale oval in the darkness, shrugged. "Guess I've always had a soft spot for stray kittens and fools. When Abe told me what you were doing, I decided you needed help—fast. Packed some lunch, filled my canteen and took out. The ranch is only about fifteen miles or so from here . . . Have you seen anything at all of your father?"

Jake shook his head. "No. Earlier on I got a lot closer to the camp—could see everything good. There's nobody around but Apaches. They started getting restless after sundown, so I figured I'd best move before one of them stumbled onto me. That's what I was doing when you showed up."

Noises were coming from the *rancheria*—pounding, yells, laughter—along with the smell of smoke and roasting meat.

"What would you have done if one of them had spotted you?" Letty asked. "You couldn't fight the whole bunch."

"Wouldn't have tried. Just explained what I was doing

here—looking for my pa—and done my best to talk my way out."

"How? Can you speak Apache or Spanish? And I've got my doubts there's one person in the whole tribe who would know enough English to understand you."

Jake, moving forward to get a better look at the camp, now all flickering firelight and shadows, smiled. The girl's interest in his well-being and problems amused and pleased him. He had thought of her several times after leaving the Kellen ranch, and had hoped they would meet again one day, but considering Tom Kellen's attitude he'd had doubts that such would ever come to pass.

"I reckon I could somehow make them understand me. Wasn't aiming to get caught, anyway," Benedict said. "And once Pa showed up I'd let him do the talking to them." He paused, considered Letty curiously. "Sure surprises me some to see you. The way your pa laid down the law I never expected to be talking to you again. He know you're here?"

"Probably does by now. He didn't know I was going to do it, if that's what you mean."

There was very little happening in the Apache camp other than eating, Benedict saw. Small groups of Indians could be seen gathered about the numerous fires partaking of their meal while the dogs waited patiently nearby for the scraps they felt would be tossed to them. Jake hoped the Apaches would keep their fires burning. Fritz Benedict, in an effort to avoid the army patrol and Sheriff Dirksen's posses, would most likely make his move at night when darkness would enable him to travel unseen. Unless the Apaches kept their camp well lit up, he'd have trouble seeing his father arrive. And he couldn't depend on hearing the wagon; he was too far from the camp.

"Sorry if I put trouble between you and your pa," Jake said, as Letty stepped in beside him.

"None that wasn't already there," she said, pressing a sandwich of bread and meat into his hand. "Time we ate a little. You haven't, have you?"

"No. Was just thinking about digging into my saddlebags for something when it came to me that I'd better move. This for sure hits the spot," he added, gesturing with the sandwich.

They ate in silence for several moments, and then Benedict said, "You coming here to find me—maybe help—that mean you believe me?"

Somewhere deep in the grove a night bird called forlornly. Letty listened for a bit, and then nodded. "Yes, I do. And I want to help you prove it."

"It's going to put you on the outs with your pa—"

"I've thought of that, and it doesn't matter," Letty said. "I'm twenty years old, and I can do as I please. I won't be able to go back home probably—unless I get down on my knees and beg him to forgive me, and I sure won't ever do that. But I'll make out."

Jake grinned. "If worst comes to worst, you could marry me and go into horse ranching," he said jokingly.

"Sure an idea," Letty replied, "one I'll keep in mind. But we better get out of this tight spot before we talk about much else. Risky hanging around here. What are you aiming to do?"

"Already said it—figure to stay put, keep an eye on the Apaches. Pa'll show up sooner or later if this is the bunch of Indians he aims to sell those rifles to."

Letty, finished with her sandwich, studied him thoughtfully. "You talk now as if you're convinced it was your pa that hijacked those guns."

"About it, I reckon. Just sort of got around to believing it. Pretty hard not to the way things shape up. Only thing I figure I can do now is try and talk him out of dealing them to the Indians."

"You'll have to head him off before he gets here then. Once he shows up they'll—"

"I realize that, but there's not much else I can do but watch and wait, and try to get to him first."

"Perhaps you're right," Letty said, staring out over the level expanse that fronted the Apache *rancheria.*

The stars and moon were not yet out in sufficient strength to light up the flat clearly, and it was now little more than a gray world of indistinguishable shadows.

"Scares me a bit, you coming here alone," Jake said. "Weren't you afraid of being seen—and caught by some of the braves?"

"I suppose so, but I didn't let it worry me. I don't think they'd do anything. They know I'm Tom Kellen's daughter, and Papa's given them a few beeves from time to time when the winters were bad and they were short on something to eat."

"Could say they were friends of his then—"

"As friendly as Apaches ever get. I speak Spanish, same as Papa. They seem to respect us for that."

"What about Apache?"

Letty shook her head. "I'm lost when they use their native tongue. Can never make heads or tails of what they're saying. I don't suppose you speak anything but English."

"That's all. Got acquainted with a few words of Spanish while I was riding across Texas on my way here, but that's it."

Letty smiled, bewildered. "Still can't understand how you expected to get anywhere with the Apaches when you don't speak Spanish—or their language—"

"Like I said, I was leaving it up to Pa."

Some sort of disturbance had broken out in the camp. Yells filled the night, accompanied by much barking from the dogs. Jake and Letty moved forward a bit to where they could see better, and put their attention on the center of the cleared ground where a large fire blazed. They could see two of the braves wrestling back and forth, each striving to throw the other off his feet.

"A fight over something," Jake guessed.

"Could be all in fun," the girl said. "They like to wrestle and scuffle about—show off their strength."

Benedict, keeping a wary eye out for danger while speaking in a low, cautious tone, shook his head. "I didn't figure Apaches ever thought of anything but raiding and killing—"

"It's a way of life for them, I guess," Letty said, "but they're not like that all the time. We had a man working for us who grew up among them. He said the most important thing to an Apache was to be brave and daring, and never show any weakness—and that's how we see them. But they do have a home life of sorts.

When they're in camp they play games, have contests, act a lot like white people do."

"Never thought of them that way," Jake said. "Got the idea from somewhere that all they ever did was make war on the settlers and pilgrims, and anybody else who wasn't an Apache."

"Expect it was that way at first when the white people moved in and took over their land . . . I've been thinking—"

She hesitated. Jake, waiting for her to finish, turned toward her. Concern was rushing through him. "What? Did you hear something?"

"No, just that I think we're in the wrong place if you're planning to intercept your father before he gets here with those rifles."

"Maybe, but we can't risk getting any closer to the camp. Besides, I've got the flats in front of me. That gives me a long view of anybody coming or going."

"I suppose—but I think you're watching the wrong direction."

"Meaning what?"

"I believe your father is holed up somewhere in the Sacramentos with those guns. There are a lot of canyons and deep washes all filled with brush that a team and wagon could easily be hidden in."

"The Sacramentos," Jake echoed thoughtfully. "They're the mountains north of here. What makes you so sure Pa's hiding out there?"

"The army and the sheriff's posses haven't been able to find him anywhere else. It's the only logical place left."

"Expect they've looked there, too—"

"Probably, but anybody wanting to stay out of sight could do it easy up there. I think we ought to move, find us a spot on the other side of the *rancheria* where we'd be between it and the mountains. We'd see your father first then—before the Apaches did—if he comes from that direction."

Benedict agreed. "We'll take the horses, swing wide around the Indians, and make a stand like you say somewhere between them and the mountains." It was a bit of good fortune having Letty at his side. She was smart and thought of things that, being a stranger to the country and the Apaches, never occurred to him. "I'll get the horses. We'd best lead them for a ways."

Taking up the leathers of the bay, and passing those of the buckskin she was riding to Letty, Jake struck off quietly into the brush, working deeper among the trees and thickets as they circled the Apache camp.

Shortly they were abreast of the collections of wickiups. The shouting and laughing indicated that whatever game was underway was still in progress, and a low, rhythmic chanting suggested that some members of the tribe were engaged in a dance of some sort.

"Careful," Jake warned, as the sounds grew louder.

It was difficult making their way through the dense growth in the pale light. Time and again Benedict led them into a blind alley of brush, and was forced to backtrack to avoid the tough, springy growth.

Finally, beyond the *rancheria,* they began to veer more toward the flat. He'd get a couple of miles or so above the camp and halt, Jake figured; such would allow ample time to intercept his father and the wagonload of guns before the Apaches caught sight of him.

Benedict came to a sudden stop as a startled cry broke from Letty Kellen's lips. Two Apache braves, one armed with a rifle, the other a bow and arrow, were facing them in the small clearing they had entered.

⇒ 11 ⇐

JAKE reacted instantly. Dropping the bay's reins, he swung his rifle like a club at the nearest brave—the one with the gun. The barrel skidded off the Apache's shoulder, thudded into his head, and knocked him to his knees. Before Benedict could wheel the other brave dropped his bow, drew a knife, and lunged at him.

Jake threw himself to one side, caught the Apache by the arm and tried to shake the knife from the man's hand. But the brave, strong and wiry, held on to the blade while struggling mightily to break free. Abruptly he succeeded and made a grab for the rifle his companion had dropped. He was successful in that also. Snatching up the weapon, he spun to face Benedict.

A fleeting glimpse told Jake that Letty had wheeled and drawn her own rifle from the saddle boot. She moved in to use it as a club on the first brave, as Jake came slowly to his feet and closed in on the Apache leveling the weapon at him. Catching the barrel, he wrenched the gun to one side, and struck out again with his rifle. The Indian grunted and fell back a step. Benedict, still hanging tight to the Apache's weapon, lashed out again with his own. At that moment Letty's voice

93

checked him.

"Jake—behind you!"

Benedict wheeled. Three more Apaches were standing just within the clearing—two with drawn bows, the third with a cocked and leveled rifle.

Jake swore deeply and, allowing his weapon to fall to the ground, raised both hands. Immediately the brave with the gun spoke to the man at his left who stepped forward and retrieved the weapon. The other two braves, now recovered, were on their feet glaring angrily at Jake and Letty. Suddenly the first man Benedict had encountered loosed a torrent of words, and drawing a knife, started for Jake. The latecomer with the rifle halted the brave with a guttural command and, pointing off in the direction of the Apache camp, motioned for Letty and Jake to move out.

Activity in the *rancheria* ceased immediately when they stepped out of the brush and entered the firelit area where the wickiups were erected. As the braves led their captives toward one of the domelike shelters in the center of the camp, men, women, and children fell in behind and followed.

"They're probably taking us to Cobre," Letty said. "He's their chief."

"I've heard of him," Jake said. "He'd be the one my pa'd be making a deal with for those rifles."

Letty nodded. "He'd be the one all right. Do you think we ought to mention it—if it comes up?"

"Don't see as it'll make any difference—and we might learn something."

They reached the chief's wickiup and halted before it.

By then the entire village had gathered around them in a half circle. Two of the braves—the pair Jake had engaged first in the clearing—had turned to the crowd and were evidently recounting details of the capture, punctuating their remarks with many gestures.

"They speaking Spanish or Apache?" Jake asked.

"Apache, and it looks like they're making a real big story out of catching us while telling everybody just how brave they were."

Jake smiled grimly. "If those other three hadn't shown up they'd have a different yarn to tell."

The faded blanket hanging over the entrance of the chief's wickiup was pulled aside, and a squat, elderly Apache man stepped into the open.

"Cobre," Letty murmured.

The head of the Apache clan showed only a flicker of surprise in his dark eyes when he saw Letty and Benedict. His round face was lined, and there was a certain sadness to the expression that lay upon it, but there was no gentleness in his jet black eyes. He was dressed much as were most of the other men—white drawers, cotton shirt, knee-high moccasins, a strip of cloth, red in this case, about his head.

Of the three braves who had come into the clearing, the one carrying a rifle stepped forward and took up a place beside Cobre. He said something to the old chief, and then to the two men who had been with him. Both came forward slowly, and reluctantly laid the rifles they had taken from Letty and Jake on the hard, sunbaked ground in front of the chief.

Cobre, arms folded across his chest, watched them in

cold silence. When the two braves had faded back into the crowd, he raised his head slightly and put his attention on Letty.

"Are you not the daughter of the man Kellen who raises cattle?" he asked in Spanish.

Letty nodded, and translated the question to Jake.

"Go ahead, talk to him," Benedict said. "You can tell me later what he had to say."

"That'll make it easier," Letty said. "As long as he speaks in Spanish, I'll be all right. If he starts talking in Apache—"

"What is it you say to your man?" Cobre broke in, frowning. "Does he not know of what we speak?"

"No, he does not. I told him that I can talk with you in Spanish but not in the Apache language."

"We will speak in Spanish," the old chief said decisively as if to preclude any opposition. Raising his eyes he gazed out over the wickiups into the smoke-filled, firelight-tinted night. There were no sounds to be heard other than the crackling of wood being consumed by flames, while the heavy odor of broiled meat still lingered in the clearing.

"Why is the daughter of Kellen and her man skulking about like coyotes around the camp of the Apache?" Cobre asked, suddenly coming back to Letty.

"We only pass by your camp," the girl replied coolly. "Your braves have made a mistake."

Cobre shook his head. "I have the word of Paco, a subchief. He says it is so. He tells me that you were both found on land that is ours. Does not the daughter of Kellen know that white people are not welcome on

Apache land? Much trouble can come from this."

"We meant you no harm. We were only passing by, as I have explained."

"Why is this?"

"We search for a certain man."

"An Apache?"

"No, the father of the man who is with me—my friend."

"This father of your friend, how is he called?"

"Fritz Benedict."

At mention of his father's name Jake glanced at Cobre. He guessed Letty was asking the chief if he knew of Fritz Benedict, but there was no change in the old Apache's stolid expression. Either he did not know of Fritz, or else he was being careful not to reveal the fact that he did.

"This man is said to be nearby?"

"We do not know. We are searching—"

Cobre said something to the man beside him, apparently Paco, the subchief, in his native tongue, and then listened patiently to the reply.

"Have you seen nothing of the man Fritz Benedict?" he asked finally.

"No," Letty said. "The chief of the Apaches speaks as if he does know Fritz Benedict. Is this a truth?"

Cobre's thin lips tightened. "Only a small one. He came to us much as a Comanchero with things to sell. We agreed to buy with gold, but he has not returned."

"Would these things you wish to buy be rifles and bullets?"

Cobre shrugged his thick shoulders, then let his small

eyes travel about the *rancheria*. The crowd that had gathered was now considerably smaller as many onlookers, finding the proceedings of no great interest, had drifted away.

"It is told me your man attacked my braves and struck them severely with his rifle," Cobre continued, slyly changing the subject.

"It is true but he did so only to defend me and himself—"

"My braves feel they must have satisfaction."

"Why is this? In the beginning there were two of them to his one. And then more came. Is it not the way of the Apache to fight bravely alone, or must he have many others to support him?"

A muttering of anger came from several braves standing nearby. Cobre silenced them with an imperious gesture.

"It is not fitting that a woman should criticize an Apache warrior," the old chief said sternly, "but I realize you speak for your man. It would be wise, however, to say no more words of the same nature . . . Where is it that you were to meet the man Fritz Benedict?"

Letty sighed, glad to be off the touchy matter of Apache male pride and on to something else.

"There was no place agreed upon. We must search until we find him."

Cobre turned his head and spat to show his contempt. "That would not be the way of the Apache. A place for a meeting would have been decided upon . . . Is this a plan of the rancher Kellen?"

"No. He knows of my friend here who is called Jake,

but he does not know what we do."

Cobre gave that consideration while he listened to words from the subchief Paco who was still standing at his side. Once during the conversation Cobre vigorously shook his head. At that point the two braves that Jake had fought surged forward angrily. The old chief waved them back and turned his attention again to Letty.

"Benito," he said, pointing to the heavier of the pair, "and Juan," he added, indicating the other, "are filled with much anger. They believe I am dealing without fairness to them if you and your man are permitted to go with no punishment."

"There is no need for punishment," Letty said. "I have told you the truth—that we meant no harm to the Apache."

"You were not spying for the soldiers?"

"No, we pass this way only in our search for Fritz Benedict. That is our true purpose, Chief Cobre."

Benito raised an arm and pointed an accusing finger at Letty and Jake. "A lie!" he shouted. "We found you sneaking as a coyote to look upon our camp!"

"It is true!" Juan declared, backing his companion. "And when we attempted to turn them away we were attacked without mercy!"

"We demand that strong punishment be administered to these trespassers!" Benito insisted. "Such would be the fate of any Apache caught spying on a white man's village."

Letty took a deep breath. "We could be in for it," she said to Benedict in a low, tense voice. "Whatever happens just stay calm—and let me handle it."

99

Jake shook his head. "If it comes down to that, I can grab up one of the rifles, jam the muzzle into Cobre's belly, and force the rest of them to back off."

"That would help us—for a couple of minutes," Letty said quietly. "We'd still never get out of here alive. Only chance is for me to keep Cobre talking, make him see things our way."

A taut hush had fallen over the Apaches while Letty and Jake exchanged their few words. Cobre, arms still folded across his thick chest, dark, swarthy features devoid of expression, did not remove his eyes from Letty.

"I do not know what was said between you and your man," he began, "but I must hear my warriors. If you are here to spy—"

"We do not spy!" Letty broke in firmly. "I have said so before, and it is true."

"Fah! A woman's word!" Juan shouted. "It is worth nothing!"

Anger colored Letty's cheeks as she faced the old chief. "I will remind you, Cobre, that the Kellens have always been a friend of the Apache. Has not my father given you beef when the winters were very cold and game was scarce? Has he not saved your people from starving many times?"

"It is so," Cobre agreed.

"Then is it not only right that my words be believed, for I am my father's daughter, and my friend and I be allowed to go on our way? Truly, we have done the Apache no harm."

"It is perhaps so. But Paco, who is a member of the

council, thinks it would be wise to make a prisoner of your man. By doing so his father would be forced to honor his words."

"You would make him a hostage?"

"Hostage? I do not know the word. We would keep him a prisoner. He would not be harmed, and he would be freed when Fritz Benedict came. Such could serve to make him hurry."

"There would be no use of such, Chief Cobre. Fritz Benedict does not know his son is here. They are as strangers."

The old chief, stoical features unchanging, turned to Paco, and in a voice loud enough for all who were nearby to hear, began to speak in Apache. He had scarcely begun when both Juan and Benito interrupted angrily. Cobre listened to their evident objections for a minute or two, and then silenced them with a sharp word and a curt slash of his hand. Several others in the crowd ceased their grumbling also.

"The daughter of Kellen and her man are free to go," Cobre said, nodding to Letty and motioning for them to retrieve their rifles. "It is wise that you get your horses and ride from here quickly. I have warned the young braves who do not understand, that the daughter of Kellen is not to be harmed, but they are headstrong and filled with anger. I will restrain them for as long as it is possible to do so. Go now."

"Many thanks, Chief Cobre," Letty said.

Coming about she signaled for Jake to head for their horses, waiting nearby. Benedict required no urging and fell in at the girl's side. Together they pushed through the crowd of sullen Apaches and reached their horses. Mounting without further delay, they rode off into the night.

## 12

"BEST WE GET BACK into the grove," Benedict said. "I don't think that pair I tangled with much liked the chief letting us go."

"They didn't," Letty said, throwing a glance over her shoulder. "Looks like they're still arguing with him about it. They'll not change his mind, however. He'll not do anything that might hurt his chances of getting a few steers from Papa if we have another hard winter."

"Maybe so," Jake said as they gained the first outcrop of brush and rocks, "but what's to keep them from taking out after us on their own?"

"Cobre's word is law among the tribe. It would be unusual if they went against him—but they could. He warned me about it."

"We'll not take any chances," Benedict said decisively, also glancing back over a shoulder. "Sort of surprised we got our guns back."

"Likely that's because I told the chief you were Fritz Benedict's son—and they're expecting to make a deal with him for those hijacked rifles."

"He come right out and say that?"

Letty nodded. "They're looking for him to show up. They had half an idea to hold you as a hostage to force your father to honor the agreement he'd made with them."

"What else did he say?" Benedict asked.

They were well within the grove now, and their mounts were picking their way along moonlit aisles between the trees and around thickets of brush. There was little sound to be heard—only the muted thud of the horses' hooves, the dry squeak of saddle leather, and the occasional click of an insect. There were no signs of game of any kind. Such led Benedict to believe that Cobre's band had hunted out the area, and as Cal Hollenbeck had said was customary with the tribes when food and firewood grew scarce, they would soon be moving on.

"It was mostly about what we were doing there, and why," Letty said, answering his question. "I think he would have let us go right away if it hadn't been for those two, Benito and Juan. Their pride had been hurt, and if they'd had their way we'd probably ended up being used for target practice."

"They were plenty worked up for sure," Jake agreed, turning his head to listen.

It was a useless motion he knew; if the two Apaches were on their trail they would be moving silently and with extreme care.

"Cobre and Paco—that subchief—are plenty up in the air over your father not showing up with those rifles," Letty said as they rode on through the crisp, silvery night. "I wonder if he's making a deal with a different tribe."

"Maybe already has," Jake said. "It's been a few days now since the hijacking, and I'd think he'd want to get the guns off his hands as soon as he could since he's got the army as well as a couple of sheriff's posses hunting for him. There many more tribes around here?"

"A few—all Mescalero Apaches."

"What about this Victorio who seems to be at the bottom of all the trouble?"

"He's over in Arizona, although he's been seen in New Mexico. Across the border in old Mexico, too." Letty paused. "He'd pay plenty to get those rifles."

"I've been wondering about that. Where do these Indians get money to buy rifles? They all look to be about as poor as Job's turkey."

"From raiding and stealing, and trading with the Mexicans—the Comancheros. Gold doesn't mean anything to them except to be used for buying rifles and cartridges from some white man."

Jake mulled that about in his mind for a long minute, then he said, "You think there's a chance Pa could have taken those guns over into Arizona, and sold them to Victorio?"

"Possibly—but it's hard to see how he could have driven the wagon that far without somebody seeing him."

"Maybe he didn't have to go clear to Arizona. Maybe Victorio and some of his braves met him around here somewhere close and took the guns off his hands."

"That's about what happened—if he made a deal with Victorio. And Victorio would have the gold to pay for them. We've heard stories of him and his braves robbing mines and holding up gold shipments for months now."

"If that's what Pa's done—turned the guns over to Victorio and his bunch—it would explain why the army and Dirksen's posses haven't been able to find him."

Letty nodded as the horses plodded steadily on. "Good chance that's it . . . I guess we were lucky to get out of Cobre's camp when we did. If he knew that he'd been double-crossed, well—we'd not be here now."

"For sure," Jake said. "I'm mighty lucky you came along. Not being able to talk to Cobre would have put me in a mighty bad spot—but you saved our necks. Can't tell you how much I'm obliged to you."

Letty's lips parted in a private sort of smile. "Expect I'm obliged to you, just for riding into 'Cruces," she said. "Where are we headed except away from Cobre's *rancheria?*"

"Trying to figure out what I ought to do now. Still need to keep an eye on Cobre's camp. Pa will show up there if he's going to deal with him. And it would be a waste of time trying to run down Victorio—especially if Pa's already handed the rifles over to him."

"That's true. Do you think there's a chance the army or one of the posses could have found your father by now, assuming he's still around?"

Benedict gave that thought. "Just could be," he said. "Might be smart to go on to the way station. Hollenbeck will know—"

Benedict's words broke off as he drew the bay up short. Letty kneed her buckskin in close to his side.

"What is it?" she asked, glancing around in the half dark.

"Heard something. Back behind us and off to the left a bit. Don't know what it sounded like. Was just a noise."

"Could it have been an animal?"

"Don't think so. The Apaches seem to have killed off all the game."

"Then it'll be some of Cobre's braves following us despite his telling them to leave us be. Most likely it'll be that pair we had trouble with, Benito and Juan."

"Good bet, but don't bank too much on what Cobre promised. Could have the same idea that Dirksen has—that if he followed me I'd lead him to my pa . . . You got any idea how far we are from open country?"

Letty, dressed now in a pair of her father's old cord pants cut down to size, plaid shirt, work boots, narrow-brimmed hat, and a red bandanna around her neck, raised herself in the stirrups and looked ahead. "Not sure but I think we're almost to the end of the grove. Can't see good enough to really tell."

"What comes then?"

"Flats," Letty replied, frowning as she attempted to accurately recall the area. "Then rocky country. Low hills and bluffs in between before you get to the Sacramentos. We're heading in the wrong direction if you want to go to the way station."

Benedict nodded. "I remembered that much, but I was figuring we could double back once we put some ground between us and the Apache camp. Don't think it'll work out that way now. Got a strong hunch that Benito and Juan, and maybe a few more, are dogging our tracks."

Letty made no comment, simply sat quietly in her saddle, and listened into the night. Abruptly she stirred, and smiled tautly at Jake. "You're right. I heard something then."

"Expect they're riding the same trail as we are. Let's get to the end of the grove and wait. If I've got to fight, I'm going to pick the place."

He moved off at once. Letty swung in behind him, and together they hurried on through the fading night. They were nearer the edge of the grove than the girl had thought, for quite suddenly they broke out into the open and were at the beginning of a broad flat. Jake at once turned back to the last stand of thick brush, and pulled off the trail. Letty, following instantly, rode her buckskin in beside his bay and dismounted. Then drawing her rifle, she moved up to where he was standing.

Weapon cradled in his arms, Jake considered her disapprovingly. "Not sure you ought to take a hand in this," he said in a whisper. He was uncertain how near the Apaches would be—ten feet or a hundred. He was equally unsure as to why they were following Letty and him—revenge or in the hope that he would take them to Fritz Benedict. "Might be you'd best stay with the horses."

"Why? I can shoot."

"Shootings what I'm going to try not to do. We don't want any gunshots that might be heard."

"But the Apache camp is miles—"

"Not thinking about them. Shots could draw the army, or some of Dirksen's deputies, if they happened to be around, and we don't want them underfoot."

"Well, I can use my rifle as a club, too," Letty pointed out. "You go ahead, set up your ambush or whatever you have in mind. I'll keep back, but if things don't go right for you, don't expect me not to step in and give you a hand."

Jake continued to study the girl. The tense, hard lines in his face softened. "I won't have you getting hurt," he said.

"Don't you think that maybe I feel the same about you?" Letty demanded promptly. And then before Benedict could speak, said, "What's your plan?"

Jake smiled, and shrugged. "You've already guessed it—an ambush. Aim to find a dark place along the trail, and wait."

"Good. We don't know how many there'll be. Two of them for sure, so I'll find a spot opposite you. First one will be yours. I'll take care of the next in case you can't get to him. If it's a big party, well—"

"If it is we let them pass. No sense taking on more than we can handle." Jake paused, a tenseness coming over him. "They're coming. Get set."

At once Letty crossed over to a thick stand of brush and took up a position behind it. Benedict, choosing a similar location a stride farther on but on the opposite side of the trail, prepared to meet the first Apache—if that was who was tracking them.

They did not have long to wait. The bobbing head of a horse as it walked at a fairly fast pace along the shadowy path abruptly came into sight. A brave was slumped on the animal's back, shoulders down, head pitched forward, legs dangling loosely against his pony's sides. At first, Jake was unable to tell who the warrior was, as the light in the grove was so faint, but as the man drew closer he recognized the brave called Benito.

Raising his rifle to use as a club, Benedict waited for the Apache to get within reach. Worry was tugging at his mind where Letty Kellen was concerned, and this distracted him somewhat. If she failed to take care of the second brave, now coming into view—and if there should be others behind him—she could find herself in real trouble. He wished now he had stuck to his original decision and made her stay clear of the ambush. But it was too late to think of that. He'd simply have to watch, and if the girl was unable to handle the brave, he'd go to her aid the instant he had finished with Benito.

The Apache following Benito wasn't Juan, Benedict saw as the rider emerged slowly from the moonlight-dappled grove into a small clearing. It was Paco, the subchief. A tightness gripped Jake. It could be as he had feared; instead of two braves seeking revenge, it could be a large party sent by old Cobre to follow them in hopes they could find Fritz Benedict. The fact that Paco was one of the party lent credence to that idea.

But, strangely, there was no one following the sub-chief. Jake briefly wondered why Benito's companion was Paco and not Juan, but he wasted no time on thought. The point was there were only two Apaches to deal with, and that was in their favor.

Benito, face still tipped down as he evidently kept close watch on the trail for any change, was in deep concentration as he drew abreast Benedict. Jake, biding his time until the exact moment, allowed the Apache to pass, and then moving swiftly, swung the stock of his rifle at the back of the brave's head.

The blow landed with shocking force. No cry of pain

escaped Benito's flaring mouth. He simply tipped sideways and began to slide from his shying horse. Benedict wheeled instantly and lunged for Paco. The Apache was jerking his pony to a stop while endeavoring to whip out his rifle and fire a bullet at Letty, rushing toward him from the shadows.

Paco's weapon never reached his shoulder. Letty, using her rifle as a prod, jammed the muzzle into the brave's ribs. Paco yelled and, recoiling to one side, lost balance on his horse and fell to the ground. Catlike, he was on his feet immediately. Spinning about he faced Jake, his teeth bared, eyes glittering as he sought to use his rifle again. He was moments too late. Swinging his gun again as a club, Benedict caught the brave solidly on the side of the head, and sent him sprawling full length.

Letty, breathing hard, a thin smile on her lips, faced Jake. "Worked out—fine."

Jake, sucking for wind also, nodded. "Did at that," he said, relief evident in his tone. "Let's get out of here. Could be more of them following. You bring up our horses while I take care of theirs."

"What can you do with them?" Letty asked, moving off.

"Scare them, send them off into the grove. It'll buy us a little time if these two wake up, or if some others come along."

"I wonder why it wasn't Juan with Benito—"

"Wondered that, too. Could be Paco was sent to keep an eye on us and Benito was along to track us if Paco lost our trail."

"That probably explains it," Letty said.

The Indian ponies frightened easily, no doubt turned skittish by the smell of a white man, and within seconds Jake had both animals pounding off into the grove.

Letty was waiting with their mounts a little beyond where the two Apaches, still unconscious, lay. Joining the girl, Jake swung up into the saddle.

"Which way?" Letty asked, kneeing her buckskin in close to him.

"Let's get to those bluffs you said were on ahead," he replied as the horses moved out. "We can head for Cornudas way station once we're sure we're in the clear."

They reached the ragged hills, and quickly rode into the maze of bluffs and arroyos. They had come fast, and after a quarter hour or so, with both horses heaving for wind, Jake pulled into a sheltered basin and halted. There he built a small fire of dry wood, and made a tin of coffee while Letty got together some of the meat and bread she'd packed before riding out to find Benedict.

Daylight was just breaking over the hills in the east when they finished their meal, and the horses were sufficiently rested. There had been no sign of Paco and Benito, or of any other Indians, and Jake reckoned they'd gotten the Apaches off their trail—at least for the time being.

Mounting, Benedict and Letty began to work their way out of the choppy hills, taking a course south for the way station. They rode in silence for the first hour, each occupied with personal thoughts. Later, after dawn, when they were moving along the sandy floor of a wash, Jake caught sight of riders well ahead, and pulled to a stop.

"Don't look like Apaches," he said as Letty drew in close on her buckskin.

She studied the distant riders thoughtfully, hand cupped over her eyes to shade them from the rising glare of the sun. "No, they don't. More like soldiers—Mexican soldiers. Some of them are wearing *sombreros* with their uniforms."

"Mexican soldiers?" Jake echoed. "Are we that close to the border?"

"No. Actually it's quite a piece, and they're not going that way either. I'd say they're headed for the Guadalupe Mountains."

Letty paused, and pursed her lips thoughtfully. "I wonder if their being here has something to do with the rumors we've been hearing about another revolution down in Mexico?"

#### ⟨⟨ 13 ⟩⟩

B ENEDICT eased back in his saddle, then shifted his weight from one foot to another. "Thought Mexico had settled down. That's what we understood back home."

"Nothing's ever really settled, it seems. I've heard Papa talking to other men about it. Benito Juarez did get the government running along all right when he took over as president, but after he died in 'seventy-two, trouble broke out again. There are a half a dozen or more factions all fighting to get control of the country. Things change so often nobody ever really knows who the head of the government is."

Jake, eyes on the party of twenty or so Mexicans slowly fading into the distance, listened in silence to the girl's words. When she had finished he pulled off his hat and thoughtfully rubbed the back of his neck.

"You reckon that bunch could have anything to do with Pa and those guns?"

Letty turned to him. "You mean they might be here to buy them?"

"Well, if that general, or whatever he is, that's leading the party is about to start a revolution or take part in one, he's probably in the market for rifles and ammunition."

Letty nodded. "That would explain why your father hasn't delivered the guns to Cobre."

"Sure would. And why else would a party of Mexican soldiers be this far inside American territory? That's not usual is it?"

"No, certainly not. I think there's an agreement between both governments to let folks go back and forth across the border for maybe a mile or so, but no farther than that."

Benedict continued to watch the riders, now little more than dark blurs on the horizon. Then he said, "I've got a hunch about this. I'll lay odds that those Mexicans are on their way right now to make a deal with Pa. Got any ideas where they might meet?"

"Could be anywhere in the Guadalupes. There are lots of deep, brushy canyons. It's sort of known as a hideout for rustlers and horse thieves."

"Could be that's where Pa's been ever since the hijacking—"

"I'm sure the army and Sheriff Dirksen's posses have

all been there looking for him, but he could easily have given them the slip. I was there once with Papa and some of the cowhands looking for stolen cattle. Never found them, but we're pretty sure they were there somewhere."

"Can bet that's right where we'll find Pa," Jake said, raking the bay with his spurs. "Let's go."

He hadn't asked Letty if she were willing to make the long ride to the Guadalupes, but had simply assumed that she would be. Jake realized this as they moved out of the wash, and struck east across a flat.

"Maybe you're tired of all this chasing around," he said, "and would as soon head on back home."

"Staying with you suits me fine," she said with a smile.

"But won't your pa be wondering and worrying where you are, and be sending some of his crew out to find you?"

"Maybe, but I doubt it. Papa's sort of given up on me—and he knows by now that I'm with you."

"How could he if—"

"I told Candy to tell him. And warn him."

"Warn him?"

Letty shrugged. "I want Papa to let me be. I'm old enough to be on my own and do what I please."

"It's kind of unusual for a girl to take off like that," Jake said. "Anyway, you just can't turn your back on your pa."

"Why can't I? If I was the son he always wanted, I'd be out on my own by now."

Benedict said, "Yeah, reckon so."

They were moving steadily east, and the Mexicans were again visible although no more than indefinite shapes in the long distance.

"You don't sound like you agree," Letty said.

"It's not the same," Jake said. "I can see where a man would feel different about a daughter and a son."

"How?"

Benedict rubbed at his jaw. "Never having been married, I sure don't claim to be no expert, but I expect a man would figure a son—being a man—could handle himself in a tight spot without any problem."

"And a daughter couldn't?" There was an edge to Letty's tone.

Jake slid her a sidelong glance. "Now, hold on! I don't want to get crossways with you about this. Like I said, I'm no expert. But it seems to me a man just naturally would want to look out for his daughter, sort of protect her, and see that she got the best. And he'd be anxious about her anytime he wasn't sure she was all right."

Letty was silent for a time while she thought over what Benedict had said. Finally, she said, "I suppose you're right, at least partly. I guess I never thought about it in that way."

"Having a pa to worry about you, and look after you seems to me would be a good thing. I was never around mine enough to really get acquainted with him. He was always sort of coming or going, and those last few years with him off chasing moonbeams all over the country, I just gave up on him."

"But you came here looking for him—"

"Yeah, sure did, and I'm not certain just why. Ma had

died hoping Pa would send for us like he had always promised, or that at least he would come home. He never did either one. And after she was gone I decided to hunt him down, tell him about Ma. And maybe throw in with him on this horse ranch idea he wrote us about. But that turned out like all the other dreams he had— plain nothing to it."

"Do you hate him for the way he's been?"

"Not sure how I feel about him. Maybe it doesn't matter one way or another. I just want to stop him from selling those guns to the wrong people if I can, not so much for his sake but for that of the folks who'll be hurt by his doing it."

Benedict shook his head as if wanting to dismiss the subject. The Mexicans appeared to be veering more to the north, evidently heading for the upper end of the rough-looking range.

"There any way we can get to those mountains without them spotting us?" he asked.

"Pretty much open country all the way," Letty replied, studying the distant riders. "Looks like they're headed for Crow Flats—or maybe even the Peak, farther north. We could start working our way toward the upper end of the mountains, and come in above them. If we keep to low ground and stay behind the rocks and brush as much as possible, it could be they won't notice us."

"Let's do it," Benedict said at once. "Unless I miss my guess those soldiers'll lead us right to Pa."

Both Letty and Jake were right. The Mexican officer, resplendent in red-and-blue piped with gold braid, and his party of soldiers, which upon closer inspection also included an American wearing a high-peaked, Texas hat, rode directly to a level, grassy plain in the rocky hills where a spring made an appearance, and there halted. All were grouped about the water hole, taking their ease in the late afternoon, when Jake and Letty, having made an approach from above, drew in behind a rocky mound a hundred yards or so north of them.

"Looks like they're expecting to meet with somebody, all right," Benedict said, as he and Letty dismounted.

"I hope for your sake it's your pa they've come to meet. Could be they're here to buy cattle from some rustler."

"I reckon we'll know soon."

But it was a good two hours before they saw a man appear suddenly at the upper end of the canyon in which the spring lay. At once Jake worked his way forward through the rocks and brush to where he could get a closer look at the new arrival. He was a dark-faced, somewhat heavyset individual wearing a baggy brown suit and crumpled gray hat.

"That your pa?" Letty asked, crawling in next to Jake and sprawling out beside him.

The tense anticipation that gripped Benedict was slowly ebbing away as he searched in vain for some indication, some clue that the man he was looking at, admittedly a fair distance away, was his father.

"I don't know," he said resignedly. "Guess I wouldn't recognize Pa if he walked right up to me. But I reckon that's him, all right," he added, and pointed to a small flat farther up the canyon. "There's the wagon."

Letty turned her attention to the vehicle halted on a

strip of level ground no more than a stone's throw away. The driver, Fritz Benedict, if that was who the man walking down to meet the Mexican soldiers was, had been unable to drive the wagon any nearer the camp because of the rough terrain, and was being forced to leave it on level ground.

"There's a chance that's not the hijacked wagon," Letty pointed out. "Lots of them around . . . Still say it could be a rustler outfit here to sell beef to the Mexicans."

"Only one way to find out about that," Jake said, pulling back. "Let's circle around and have a look at what it's loaded with. We'll know then for sure."

⇢🟐 14 🟐⇠

G ETTING CLOSER to the wagon was no problem. In the fading daylight Jake and Letty made their way back to the horses, mounted and, rounding a shoulder that jutted out from a major formation of the Guadalupes, were able to draw within only a few strides of the vehicle. Leaving their saddles at that point, they continued the remainder of the way, crouching low as they moved through the rocks and brush.

The wagon, a red-wheeled hard-tail with a tarp spread over its bed, was hitched to a team of sturdy Morgans. It had been halted at the head of the canyon in which the Mexicans had made camp. Whether by design or accident, the place chosen by Fritz Benedict would not permit his taking the vehicle any nearer, as the narrow flat where he had halted broke off in a sheer drop of considerable height. Most likely, Jake guessed, Benedict had planned it so; he was taking no chances on another hijacking—one in which he would be the victim.

"Let's get in closer. Got to see what's under that tarp," Jake said, glancing toward the camp.

The men were all standing about the fire. Several bottles of liquor had been produced and were making the rounds. In the clear, closing darkness the sounds of their voices carried up the canyon, rousing faint echoes when a loud burst of laughter punctuated their conversations.

"We'd better go now," Letty said as she hunched beside Jake, crouched behind a large boulder. "That officer will want to take a look at the rifles—if that's what's in the wagon—before he does any buying."

Jake nodded, drew himself erect, and prepared to hurry across the last few yards that separated them from the hard-tail. Letty caught at his arm and stayed him.

"Too late," she said. "They're coming—three of them."

Benedict was already dropping back into a crouch, his eyes again turned to the camp. The Mexican officer, the man wearing the tall hat, and the driver of the wagon were picking their way slowly up the canyon. Strong tension was building within Jake. At last he would be getting a look at his father, his first look in years. Would he recognize him?

"I wish to hell I was a bit closer," he muttered, watching the men approach. "Getting darker. Going to be hard to see."

"You don't dare move," Letty said, her voice rising

with alarm. "They'll spot you sure."

Jake nodded. He would have to be satisfied with where he was, and if luck was with him he should not only be able to see all the men fairly well, but hear what they would be saying as well.

Yells broke out down at the camp, and the men paused to look back. Two of the soldiers were locked in each other's arms, swaying and stumbling about in what appeared to be a good-natured wrestling match. The Mexican officer and the two men with him watched for a few moments, and then resumed the climb up the steep slope.

"What do you aim to do?" Letty asked.

"Sit tight," Jake answered. "Only choice we've got."

The scuffling and shouting was still going on down in the camp, but Jake gave the disturbance no more attention. He centered his glance on the three men, now becoming more distinct in the evening haze.

"That's Colonel Melindrez," Letty said suddenly, in a surprised voice. "I remember him."

"Sure wearing a fancy outfit," Jake murmured. "You meet him somewhere?"

"Yes, at the ranch. He came by a few weeks ago to see Papa. Wanted to buy cattle."

"Who do you reckon the one in the big hat is? Sure doesn't look Mexican," Jake commented.

"No, he's an American, all right. Probably a Texan from the way he's dressed. You think he could be a partner of your father's?" Letty asked.

"Maybe. Pa once mentioned a partner. He could have gone after this Colonel Melindrez, and brought him here to meet Pa."

"Or he could be somebody Melindrez brought along himself to interpret for him. I remember the Colonel didn't speak any English . . . What about the other man? Do you think he's your father?"

"Still can't say—"

The men had reached the wagon. Fritz Benedict, circling to the rear, untied a corner rope, and threw the canvas aside. Reaching into one of several crates, he drew out a rifle and handed it to Melindrez.

"Guess that settles it," Letty murmured. "It's the hijacked guns, all right."

Taut, Jake watched the Mexican officer lift the weapon to his shoulder, sight along its barrel, and experimentally work the lever as if jacking a cartridge into the chamber. What slim hopes Jake Benedict might have entertained that his parent was not involved in the stealing of the rifles and ammunition was dispelled in that moment. Not that he had seriously considered such a possibility after talking with Cal Hollenbeck at the way station; but as is always the case when a man doesn't want to accept an unpleasant truth, hope still persists within him until finally he is faced with an irrefutable bit of evidence, and there is no further possibility of denying the inevitable.

The man in the tall hat said something in Spanish to Melindrez as he took the weapon from him. The officer made a reply, after which the American turned to Benedict.

"The Colonel says this here's a real fine gun, just what he's wanting," he said in a voice thick with a southern accent. "But he's got to see what's in the rest of the boxes. Aims to make sure they're filled with new repeating rifles just like this one."

The man in the brown suit shrugged, and muttered something unintelligible as he climbed up into the wagon. Taking a hatchet, he began to pry off the tops of the crates. When that was done, he sat down on the side of the wagon bed.

"There you are, Colonel," he said, motioning to the officer. "Help yourself. You won't find nothing but brand-new guns in them boxes, just like I claimed."

Jake leaned forward, eyes searching the dark features of the man as he sought to verify in his mind the identity of his father.

Melindrez climbed up into the wagon, and went about methodically inspecting the contents of each crate. Finished with that he turned again to the Texan, and once more said something in Spanish.

"The Colonel wants to see the shells," the man with the drawl relayed.

The man in the brown suit reached for the hatchet and, moving to one of the small boxes, loosened the lid and pushed it back to reveal its contents. Melindrez smiled and, reaching a hand into the mass of loose, brass cartridges, stirred them about for a bit, and then drew back, satisfied. Directing more words to the interpreter, he dismounted from the wagon.

"Everything's fine the Colonel says," the Texan reported. "Wants you to come on back to camp and he'll figure out a deal—"

"The hell with that—there ain't no figuring to be

done! He knows my price and I ain't budging one copper from it," Benedict declared. Picking up the hatchet, he started to nail the tops of the boxes into place. "Plenty of other buyers around here just aching to get their hands on them repeaters, a bunch of Apaches, for one. And they ain't far from here, so it won't be no big chore to turn my rig about and drive over to their village."

The Texan duly translated Fritz Benedict's heated remarks to Melindrez. The officer made a lengthy reply, and then turning on a heel, abruptly started down the slope for the camp.

"Ain't no use for you to fret none, friend," the interpreter said, watching the officer leave. "Ain't no cause to get all riled up. The Colonel aims to pay your price, he just says it ain't civilized to do business up here in the dark. Wants to handle everything down there where there's light so's a man can see—and there's plenty of tequila to drink. Anyway, the gold he'll be paying you off with is in his saddlebags."

Benedict had finished replacing the tops of the wooden crates and boxes, and was listening in silence.

"What do you say?" the Texan pressed.

Fritz Benedict dropped from the wagon bed, jerked the canvas cover back into place, and dusted his hands. "Well, if that's what the Mex wants then I reckon it's all right with me. Only I don't want no fooling around," he added, patting the holstered pistol at his side suggestively.

"Don't fret about that, Benedict," the man in the tall hat said. "You'll get paid off—in gold."

J AKE settled back in the rocks. He'd had his look at his father, and now a heaviness filled him. "So that's my pa," he murmured.

"Did you get a good look at him?" Letty asked.

"Good enough. Not much like I remember him."

Letty continued to watch the two men as they picked their way down the slope. They had all but caught up with Colonel Melindrez.

"I'm sorry, Jake," she said after a while. "I was hoping it might turn out different, that it wouldn't be him."

Benedict shrugged. "Obliged to you for all your help. Don't mind saying I needed somebody like you with me. But I ain't letting it end here. I can't undo the hijacking and the killings, but I can sure try to stop him from selling those rifles to Melindrez."

The girl turned to him. "How?"

Jake had moved to the edge of the rocks and brush, and was staring down at the camp. The fire had been replenished and now a bright glow lit up the area near the spring. There was much laughing and loud talking going on, and liquor continued to flow freely.

"Expect they'll be busy down there doing their drinking and dickering," Jake said. "Soon as they get to it, I'm going to drive that wagon back to the way station and turn the guns over to the army, to that Lieutenant Forrest. He's camped right close by."

Letty frowned. "But won't Melindrez and the rest hear?"

"Don't think so, not if I lead the team and wagon off for a ways before driving them." Jake paused. Except for the noise coming from the camp below, the night was quiet, and now filled with a pale glow from the moon and stars overhead.

"If I can do that," Benedict continued, "it will go a little ways to righting the wrong Pa has done . . . You mind looking after my horse?"

Letty smiled. "You know better than to even ask. I'll ride along behind you, sort of keep an eye out on our back trail."

"If I'm lucky there won't be no need," Jake said, and started out of the rocks for the wagon. At once he halted, and then stepped back.

"Two men coming up the slope—"

"Probably want to have a look at the rifles, too," Letty said, craning her neck to see.

"Maybe. Just could be that Mexican colonel is sending them up here to stand guard. He might be scared the Apaches, or somebody else, will come along and steal the whole lot."

Crouched among the rocks, Jake and Letty watched the two soldiers toil up the grade. Laughing and talking, one carrying a bottle by its neck, they finally reached the rim of the flat and moved toward the wagon.

Reaching the vehicle one immediately pulled back the tarpaulin and dragged the crate of rifles nearest him to the side of the wagonbed. Earlier Fritz Benedict had nailed the box shut and, mumbling angrily, the man expressed his displeasure by giving the crate a shove. His partner, standing off to one side and showing no interest in the rifles, took a swallow from the bottle he was holding and said something in Spanish.

Letty leaned forward to hear the words, and then translated them to Jake. "He told his friend not to be in a hurry, that they'd be out in the hot sun carrying those rifles soon enough."

The other Mexican laughed and pulled the tarp back into place, after which the two of them moved to a low rise at the rear of the wagon and settled down to take turns at the bottle and carry on a conversation.

Benedict swore softly. The men had been sent to guard the wagon, just as he had feared. He, with Letty's aid, would have to overpower the pair, and that would not be easy. Crouched among the rocks as they were—only a few strides from the men—they could neither back off and circle around nor leave by crawling along the sides. They would have to approach the soldiers straight on.

"Only one way we can do this," Jake said quietly, studying the soldiers, "and that's walk right up to them. I think they're too drunk to do anything until we get close. Then it'll be up to us to take over."

Letty signified her understanding and, hanging her rifle in the crook of an arm, got to her feet.

"You say something to them in Spanish," Benedict continued. "That'll throw them off guard, maybe give us more time to step in, knock them cold."

Again Letty nodded. Jake glanced off in the direction of the camp. Things appeared to be much the same there—the brightly burning fire, men standing or sitting around it while laughing and talking, the everpresent bottles of liquor being passed around.

Jake shook his head. "Probably best I handle this by myself," he said, having second thoughts about endangering Letty. "That pair's plenty drunk. I ought to be able to step right up to them and knock them out before they're over being surprised."

"Yes, I expect you could," Letty agreed, "only you're not going to try. I'll be right with you. Anyway, a woman coming up to them out of the dark will really surprise them."

Benedict studied the girl's set, determined features for a long minute while he considered her words. "All right," he said finally. "I'd feel better if you'd stay out of it, but have it your way." Again he looked toward the camp. "Let's get at it. We hold off too long some of the others might decide to come up here."

"I'm ready," Letty said and, stepping out of the rocks, fell in beside Jake.

Shoulder to shoulder they started walking toward the two soldiers. The men seemed not to notice at first, and then suddenly, as if realizing they were being approached by strangers, quickly made an effort to straighten up.

"*Alto!*" one managed to blurt out.

"*Que tal?*" Letty responded, and continuing in Spanish said, "Our horses ran from us, and we are lost. Can you tell me if there is a ranch nearby?"

The soldiers hesitated. One lowered his rifle as Jake and the girl drew up before them. "There is no ranch here," he began. Then from the corner of his eye, he saw Benedict's rifle swinging at his head and lurched to one side.

The frantic move was to no avail as the barrel of Benedict's weapon struck him along the temple. In his haste to avoid the blow, the soldier collided with his partner, who was much further into the liquor and therefore reacting with less celerity. Both men went over in a tangled heap. Jake silenced the cursing of the second man with a quick, solid rap to the head, and wheeled to Letty.

"Best we tie and gag them," he said.

Moving quickly, he jerked the bandannas from the necks of the two soldiers and, with Letty's help, tied the folded strips of cloth tightly over their mouths. Then, casting about for something with which to bind their hands, Jake cut some short lengths from the rope that held the canvas to the wagonbed and, rolling the unconscious pair onto their bellies, secured their wrists.

"I reckon that'll hold them," Jake said, stepping back. He was breathing hard from the exertion and, despite the coolness that had set in, beads of sweat lay on his forehead. He glanced at Letty.

The girl had turned her attention to the camp. There appeared to be little change; the fire continued to blaze up into the night as before, and the men were still sitting and standing around, Benedict saw. One of the party began to sing, a faltering somewhat discordant solo that disturbed the quiet. There was no sign of Melindrez, Fritz Benedict, or the Texan. Evidently they were off by themselves transacting their business.

"Nothing's changed down there," Jake said. "Let's get out of here."

Crossing quickly to the team, he took the bridle of the

near horse in his hand and, clucking softly to the animals, began to wheel the wagon about. The iron-tired wheels cut deep into the sandy soil and clicked against rocks with abnormal loudness, it seemed to Jake. He continually threw glances to the camp, fearful the Mexicans would hear, but none appeared to notice, and he completed the turnaround without incident.

Letty, in the saddle of her buckskin, holding the reins of Benedict's bay, waited until he had come fully about, and then rode in close.

"You going to drive now?"

Jake shook his head. "No, think I'll lead the team off a ways farther. You go on ahead."

Hand firmly gripping the horse's headstall, Jake began to walk. The Morgans came along obediently, showing no reluctance as they started down the slight grade for the flat.

"You get out front," Jake called to Letty, only a short distance before him in the night. "Pick the shortest way to Cornudas—and I'll follow."

Letty hesitated, waiting until he had led the team and wagon off the grade and climbed onto the seat of the vehicle. Then, moving up to the rear of the rig, she dismounted, tied Jake's bay to the iron ring in the tailgate, and returned to the buckskin.

"I guess we're all set," she said, swinging up onto her horse. There was a tenseness in her voice.

Jake grinned reassuringly at her through the half dark. "Don't worry none, we'll make it," he said. "See you at the way station!"

## ➿ 16 ➿

FOR THE FIRST MILE OR SO, Jake Benedict held the team to a fast walk while doing his utmost to avoid rough and rocky terrain. It was not too difficult a task as the night was bright and clear, and he had few problems in picking a course.

Care was absolutely necessary, Jake felt, and he was taking no chances on setting up any more noise in his passage than necessary. Sounds carried far in the high country; a sudden jolt of the wagon could start a jingling of chains and a solid thud that just might be heard back in the Mexican camp.

But once down on comparatively level ground, and far enough away from the canyon to feel safe, Jake put the Morgans to a good trot, and rapidly began to pull away from the rocky area where they had left the two soldiers bound and gagged.

He could see Letty a hundred yards ahead, picking a trail across the open country, avoiding the low hills and arroyos, endeavoring to stay on smooth prairie as much as possible as she set a course south for the way station. Occasionally she would drop back and swing in close to the wagon as if to assure herself that all was going well. One time Benedict beckoned her in alongside.

"How far to Cornudas?" he asked, raising his voice to be heard above the noise of the wagon.

Letty glanced back at the mountains. "Twenty miles, maybe a bit more."

"Ought to make it before daylight," Jake said, satisfied.

He wanted to be as far from the Mexicans' camp as possible before sunrise, and if all went well they should make it to the way station with no trouble. But such conviction was based on the premise that his father and the others would not discover the absence of the wagon for at least an hour. Should luck go against him in that, Jake knew he could be in trouble. The soldiers, giving chase on their horses, could soon overtake the heavily loaded wagon in an all-out race.

Without conscious thought, Benedict called on the Morgans for more speed, popping the whip over their sleek, muscular bodies, but never allowing the leather to touch them, as he'd learned to do on the family farm.

The farm . . . Jake's mind drifted back to the Benedict home in Tennessee. It had been hard for him to operate the place by himself—long hours of drudgery that sapped him of every ounce of strength. But he had accepted it as his lot, much as a card player does the hand dealt him. And there was always the promise of better things, that his father would be sending for him and his mother, or would himself return to take charge and assume some of the responsibilities.

Jake had wondered many times what it would have been like if Fritz Benedict had remained at home and not gone wandering off to the new frontier in search of a better life. The farm would have improved with his help, perhaps even prospered—and likely Emma Benedict would still be alive.

Fritz's prolonged absence had brought about the

breakdown in her health, Jake was certain. When month after month passed and there was no word from him, she had begun to pine, to grow listless, and finally to give up hope. In a short time she had become a prisoner of her bed—and eventually was gone. Lung fever, the town doctor had said, but Jake knew such was not the only cause; a lonely, broken heart had had much to do with it.

He had hated Fritz Benedict then for what he had done to the quiet, gentle woman who had worked so hard to make a home for her husband and son. And had Fritz shown up at the farm anytime in the first months after her death, he would have faced a bitter accounting and been made to understand that his neglect had been a major factor in the passing of Emma Benedict—something that Jake could never forgive.

But Fritz Benedict had not returned and to this day was unaware that the woman he had married some thirty years ago was dead, that the farm in Tennessee was no more, and that the son he scarcely knew who had been searching angrily for him was now endeavoring to prevent his becoming more deeply involved in breaking the law.

The team rushed on, now loping easily on a slight downgrade. They would need rest soon, Jake realized, although he would like to maintain the good pace at which they were moving for another hour or so before drawing to a halt. By then he would have put several miles between him and the Mexican camp. But it would be foolhardy to run the horses into the ground. That would end all hope of reaching Cornudas at all.

It felt good to be on the seat of a wagon again, especially one so tight and solidly built, holding the lines of a good team in his hands. It was like the days back in Tennessee, although he had never seen the time when he had a span of horses as fine as the pair of Morgans to drive.

Why couldn't his father have been truthful about his intention to raise horses? Jake could think of no better way of life than to be around horses, raising them, caring for them, and perhaps developing a prize strain that would set them apart from all other breeds. He'd always had a way with horses, and devoting his time to breeding and—

Abruptly the team shied and cut hard to the right. Jake caught a glimpse of a narrow but deep wash directly ahead, and the dark, lean shape of a coyote or wolf bolting from its brushy depths. In the next moment the wagon was going over. Dropping the lines, Jake threw himself off the seat, breathing a silent prayer that he would land clear of the capsizing vehicle.

He struck solid ground only slightly beyond the wagon. Wheels spinning madly, it came to rest at a canted angle, contents scattered badly while the team, restrained by their strong leather harness, stood close by heaving and trembling.

"Are you hurt?"

Letty's voice brought Jake about. He was on his feet in the center of the spilled cargo looking around. One of the crates had broken open. Rifles were everywhere, some partly buried in the loose sand. A wooden box of brass cartridges had also burst on impact, and the bullets lay in an irregular pile gleaming softly in the pale light.

Jake rubbed at his shoulder, which was throbbing slightly. "Nothing wrong with me," he said, and turned at once to the wagon. "Got to get this thing back on its wheels and loaded again. No time to lose."

Grasping the edge of the wagonbed and pulling down, Jake put his strength into righting the overturned vehicle. It hardly moved at all. Sturdily built of hickory, oak, and strap iron, it was much heavier than an ordinary wagon of similar size.

"We'll have to use your rope and horse," he called to Letty. "May take the bay, too," he added, glancing at the gelding which had come loose from the vehicle's tailgate when the accident occurred.

The girl, shaking out her lariat, handed the loop end to Benedict and then drew off a short distance. Running the rope across the wagonbed, Jake hooked it onto one of the underbraces and, stepping back, motioned to Letty.

"Pull!" he yelled.

At once Letty raked the buckskin with her spurs. The rope, dallied about the horn of her saddle, snapped taut, and with Jake again putting his weight into the effort, the vehicle flipped back over onto its four wheels.

"Next thing's to load up," he said, as the dust settled.

"Those crates are heavy," Letty said, now off her saddle and at his side. "Between the two of us we maybe can—"

"Expect I can handle them," Jake said, lifting the end of one of the rectangular boxes. "Something you can do, if you will. Settle my horse down and tie him to the back of the wagon again, and then pick up those cartridges and put them in their box."

Letty moved off at once to do as he asked. Jake, still holding up one end of the crate of rifles, dragged it to the rear of the wagon and, lowering the tail gate, propped it against the edge of the bed. Then, by lifting the narrow box to the proper height, he was able to slide it back into the wagon.

Following the same procedure, Benedict got the next three crates of weapons into the vehicle, and turned to the last. It lay empty, the top boards splintered, the rifles scattered about along the wash that had been the cause of the accident.

Taking up the empty box Jake returned it to a place in the wagonbed and then, collecting the rifles, carried them three and four at a time—absently brushing the sand from their dully gleaming, blue metallic surfaces as he did—and stowed them in the crate.

When that was done he moved to where Letty was finishing up with the box of cartridges and, taking over from the girl, replaced the lid on the wooden box as best he could and carried it to the wagon. The other box of ammunition had not come open when thrown from the vehicle, and it needed only to be added to the rest of the cargo.

Moving hurriedly and tight-lipped, Jake closed the tailgate, briefly examined the lead rope of the bay, again fastened to one of the rings, and then circled around to look over the still-nervous Morgans. He found the animals and their harness apparently no worse for the accident.

"I reckon we can pull out," he said, hurriedly climbing into the seat. "This cost us an hour, and I got my doubts that we can make up much of it."

Letty, mounting the buckskin, glanced toward their back trail. "No sign of anybody yet," she said, and then added, "Wagon tracks are pretty plain, though. I can see where the wheels cut into the ground for quite a ways."

"Means anybody trailing us will have an easy time of it," Benedict said. Gathering up the lines, he started the team forward with a slap of the leathers.

"We've still got a good lead on them," Letty said as she spurred on ahead of the Morgans. "I expect we can hold it."

The land became increasingly broken, Jake noted, as the team once again set itself to a steady lope. There were more small washes and ravines, and one time he found himself driving across a wide, sandy arroyo into which the iron-tired wheels of the wagon sank deep. It threw a heavy strain on the horses. But the Morgans were equal to the task, and they were soon once more up on the solid surface of the prairie, pressing steadily on toward the way station.

It was growing lighter as false dawn began to show in the sky above the Guadalupes in the east, and soon the protection of the night, effective at a distance despite the bright glow from the heavens, would be lost. Benedict had hoped to reach Cornudas way station with the wagonload of guns by daybreak, but the accident had used up valuable time. He doubted now that he could make it to the way station before his pa and the Mexican soldiers, who were most certainly aware of the wagon's disappearance by that hour. Disturbed by that probability, he caught Letty Kellen's attention and waved her in.

"How far to Cornudas?" he asked when she had swung in beside the wagon.

Letty glanced around. "Five, maybe six miles. Not far now. Why? Is there—" She broke off suddenly and pointed to their back trail. "Look!"

Benedict twisted about and followed the line of her outstretched arm with his eyes. Riders were streaming over the horizon behind them and coming on fast.

## ⇒ 17 ⇐

G O ON AHEAD!" Jake shouted to the girl. "Get to the way station—tell Hollenbeck I'm coming in with the wagon. Have the army meet me!"

Letty pulled away and, using her spurs on the buckskin, started for Cornudas at a fast gallop. Jake, whip in hand, leaned forward on the wagon seat and cracked the braided leather above the Morgans' heads. They responded at once by lunging into their harness and breaking into a hard run.

Bracing himself with legs spread, a foot firmly against each side of the wagonbed, Benedict looked back. The soldiers were gaining. They had spread out in a ragged line with Melindrez—identifiable by his ornate uniform—in the center. A little to one side was the Texan, and on beyond him was a horse carrying double. That would be Fritz Benedict sharing a mount.

Turning back around, Jake popped the whip again and yelled encouragement at the team. The Morgans increased their speed. They were crossing a near-level flat with clumps of chapparal and cholla cactus thinly scattered about presenting the only resistance, and shortly the wagon, going at top speed, began to sway from side to side.

Jake heard the thud of the heavy crates as they began to slide about in the wagonbed, and the fear of the vehicle overturning again gripped him. Taut, he threw another glance over his shoulder.

The Mexicans appeared not to have gained on him since the team had broken into a hard run. If he could hold them at their present pace, and not wreck the wagon, he had a good chance of making it to the way station—assuming it was not too much farther.

Steadying himself, one hand on the side-rail of the seat, feet still apart and wedged against the sides of the vehicle, Jake looked ahead. A smoke streamer was hanging in the sky not too far in the distance. That would be the way station. Where the hell was the damned army? There should be some sign of Forrest and his cavalrymen coming to meet him by then.

Jake brushed impatiently at the sweat on his forehead and swore again. Maybe he wasn't allowing enough time. It could be that Letty hadn't reached Cornudas yet, or was just now doing so. And, too, it would take a few minutes for Forrest to get his men mounted and on the way.

They had better show up soon, Benedict thought grimly, again looking back at Melindrez and his soldiers. The Morgans, strong and tough as they were, could not continue to run at full speed for much longer, and once they started to slow, it wouldn't take long for the officer and his men to catch up.

The wagon hit a prairie dog mound of sunbaked soil, then bounced and reeled drunkenly. Benedict, almost thrown from the careening vehicle, hauled back on the reins, slowing the team as he struggled to get the wagon again under control and rolling forward on a straight course.

The vehicle soon settled down, and the tireless Morgans resumed their headlong race across the prairie. Jake stared anxiously beyond their bobbing heads. The smoke plume was much nearer and more definite, and a small dark smudge on the horizon had appeared and was steadily growing larger. Cornudas way station.

Spirits lifting, Jake ventured a look over his shoulder. His mouth tightened. Melindrez and his men were much nearer—alarmingly so. He had lost ground when the wagon had struck the mound of dirt and gone out of control, and he had been forced to slow the team in order to keep from overturning. The soldiers would soon be within rifle range.

Benedict swore again in exasperation. Where was Lieutenant Forrest and his men? They should be in sight by now. Plenty of time had elapsed for Letty to have reached the way station and for the cavalrymen to have ridden out. There was no sign of them, however—no blur of oncoming horses in the distance, no dust cloud stirred up by their hoofs.

A faint, hollow crack reached Jake's ears. Gunfire. The Mexicans had begun to shoot at him, no doubt hopeful of getting in a lucky shot and hitting one of the horses, or him. They were still too far out of range to worry about, but they were closing the gap.

In the next few moments it became apparent to Jake Benedict that the Morgans were beginning to tire. Their extended, straining necks were lifting slightly, and the wild, headlong speed they had maintained was slackening. A quick look back told Jake that Melindrez and his riders, their horses unhampered by a heavily loaded wagon, were now gaining rapidly.

More gunshots sounded, the reports still sounding distant, but now spurts of sand began to show behind the wagon, and then, within only moments it seemed to Jake, along both sides.

There was still no sign of Forrest. It was evident now to Benedict that the officer and his squad of cavalrymen would not be coming. Likely they were off somewhere searching for Fritz Benedict and the wagonload of stolen guns. It was ironic that while he was doing so, the man and the hijacked weapons were being delivered to him.

A bullet struck the handrail of the seat, and screamed off into space. Melindrez and his men were close. They would soon be in a position to stop him—either by shooting one of the Morgans, or putting a bullet into him. But the way station wasn't too far now, he saw. The smudge of buildings had taken shape, could be no more than a mile distant. Wrapping the lines about a leg, Jake picked up the rifle lying on the floorboard and, twisting about, emptied it at the oncoming Mexican soldiers. There was no time to aim; he simply fired all the cartridges in the Henry rifle in the general direction of Melindrez and his men in the hope of slowing them down.

Dropping the weapon, Jake put his attention again on the lagging team. He had never been a man to punish a horse, but now he had no choice; he must reach the way station at any and all costs. Going to the whip again, he laid it on the Morgans' broad hindquarters, calling for their best—and possibly their last—as bullets began to peck at the bed of the wagon, and whir past Jake's head. The team responded. The vehicle seemed to spurt ahead, gain speed. Once again it began to sway from side to side on the long slope that led down to the way station.

Benedict set his jaw, and crouched low on the seat of the careening wagon. If the team could hold out for another quarter mile, if none of the Mexicans' bullets found their mark in him or one of the horses, he'd have it made. He knew it was a big if. But shortly a hard grin split his dry lips. He saw Letty standing beside Cal Hollenbeck near the open gate of the corral. Both had a rifle in their hands, and as he swept by in a boiling cloud of dust and entered the pole-fenced yard, both began to fire at the oncoming riders.

Pulling the heaving, foam-flecked team to a halt, Jake seized his rifle and, leaping from the wagon, hurried past the frantic bay gelding rearing and fighting the rope that held him prisoner to the vehicle, and closed the gate.

"Where's that lieutenant?" he yelled, joining Letty and the station agent as he thumbed cartridges from his bandoleer into the magazine of his weapon.

"Somewhere out there hunting that wagon!" Hollenbeck answered through the drifting dust and powder smoke. "Let's get inside the station. Them Mex mean business!"

Jake, rifle loaded, cast a look at Letty. Her eyes mirrored the relief she felt at seeing him safe and unharmed. He grinned at her and, with Hollenbeck leading the way and Letty in front of him, beat a hasty retreat to the way station's main building, firing at the soldiers as they did. Reaching the entrance and darting inside, Hollenbeck slammed the heavy plank door shut and cropped the crossbar into the iron brackets to secure it.

"Pick yourself a rifle port or a window," the station agent said, his voice high and light with excitement.

"Where's your swamper?" Jake asked.

"Jose? Oh, he's off visiting his family . . . You figure we ought to close the shutters?"

"Better leave them open so we can see," Jake replied, crossing to where he could look out and see the wagon and the still-heaving team. "Going to have to keep an eye on the corral. There another gate in the back?"

"Nope, only that'n in the front," Hollenbeck replied, stationing himself at one of the ports near the door and opening fire.

Having but one entrance to the corral to guard would help, Jake thought. He glanced about for Letty. She was standing behind him reloading her rifle. She looked up, saw his eyes on her, and smiled.

"I want you to keep away from the windows. Use one of the ports," he said. "Expect we're in for it good," he added as a hail of bullets smashed into the wall of the building. "Don't want you getting hurt."

Letty's smile widened. "Would it make a difference to you if I did?"

The clatter of glass breaking and falling to the floor as

a bullet shattered one of the front panes caused Benedict to turn quickly and look in the direction of the noise.

"Bet on it," he said, coming back around to her. "Got plans for us—if we get out of here alive."

Bullets thudded into the door, cutting off any more words that he may have intended to say. Again glass tinkled as a slug destroyed another window. Hollenbeck began to curse in a steady, harsh stream, and fire his weapon as fast as he could work the lever. Jake, pivoting, hurried through the smoke and dust that was beginning to fill the room to the port in the wall facing the corral, and peered out. The sudden assault on the door could be a diversion, something to draw attention while several of the soldiers tried to reach the wagon and drive it off.

He had guessed right. Two of Melindrez' men rode in close. Both left their saddles in a long jump and legged it for the gate. Jake took quick aim at one and dropped him in midstride. He triggered a second shot at the other soldier. The bullet was low and caught the man in the leg, sending him to one knee. Casting a fearful look at the port on the wall of the way station as if expecting another, more final bullet, he dragged himself about, seized the stirrup of one of the horses. Half running and half dragging, he made his way back to the rest of Melindrez' soldiers, who were riding back and forth and firing steadily at the way station.

Jake moved over to where Hollenbeck, still muttering curses, was maintaining an answering fire. From there he could see two of the Mexicans were down and one of the horses had been hit. Melindrez himself, with Fritz Benedict and the Texan, had pulled together near center of the milling riders, and were talking over matters. All three were out of range, and, as the man Jake wounded approached the other soldiers, the rest fell back to a safe distance, too.

"Can save your ammunition," Jake said, turning to face Letty and the station agent. "They've backed off, at least for now."

"Just hashing over what they'll try next," Hollenbeck said, taking advantage of the lull to reload his rifle. He paused, looking closely at Jake through the haze. "Expect you've done thought of this, but us a'shooting blind like we are at that bunch, one of us could kill your pa. Might even be you that'd hit him."

Benedict, refilling the magazine of his gun also, shrugged. He hadn't given the possibility any consideration, and strangely for a son, he supposed, it didn't seem to matter. But then there had never been anything between him and Fritz Benedict—only the knowledge that one was the father, the other the son. There was little beyond that.

"I reckon it don't make any difference," he said, finally. "He picked being an outlaw—nobody made him do it. And what happens to him is no concern of mine. What I'm trying to do now—keeping him from selling those guns he stole and giving them back to the army— is for Ma's sake. Anyway, he could be the one who puts a bullet in me."

There was silence for a long minute, and then Letty said, "I doubt he even knows you're in here."

Jake's wide shoulders stirred again. "He's never known much of anything about me. I used to think he did, that he sort of cared about me, but since I came down here and found out the kind of man he is—and probably has been all the time—I've marked him off . . . How're you both fixed for cartridges?" he added, taking off the now empty bandoleer and tossing it aside.

"I'm just about out," Hollenbeck said, rummaging about in his pockets.

"I've got maybe a dozen," Letty reported.

"About to run out myself," Jake said. "Got an extra box in my saddlebags, but they won't do us any good out there." Pausing, he glanced around the room. "There a back door to this place?"

"Sure, that one there behind the counter—"

"Can I get to the corral through it?"

"Yeah, reckon you can, but if you're thinking what I figure you are, you best forget it. Them jaspers out there will never let you—"

"Going to have to take a chance on that. Only hope of holding them off until the army shows up is to get us a box of that ammunition in the wagon."

"Guess you're right. Is it the same caliber as what we're shooting?"

"It could be different. I'd best grab up three of the rifles while I'm out there."

"You'll need help doing all that," Letty said, propping her rifle against the wall and moving toward him. "I'll go, and you can pass the guns to me through—"

"I'll give him a hand," Hollenbeck cut in. "The two of us can get it all done quick."

Jake was shaking his head even before the station agent had finished speaking. "No, I need both of you to give me cover. Soon as I get outside open up on them—try and keep them back where they are if you can."

"That ain't going to be easy," Hollenbeck said, stepping up to the port he was using and peering out. "They'll be watching, and from where they are they'll dang sure see you."

Jake was looking at Letty. She had moved closer, her eyes filled with care, features taut with worry.

"Isn't there some other way—something else we can do? I—I don't want you going out there."

Laying his rifle on a nearby table, Jake took the girl in his arms and held her close. Then, lowering his head, he kissed her on the lips.

"Don't fret none about me. I'll be all right. And if there's going to be any you and me in the days to come, we're going to have to make it through this," he said, and pivoting, started for the door in the back wall.

Letty had turned away also and, adding Jake's rifle to her own, hurried to one of the ports.

"Say the word," Hollenbeck called, "and me and the lady'll start cracking down on them jacklegs!"

Jake reached the door, slid the bolt, and taking the knob in hand, drew the panel back. Hesitating, he glanced over a shoulder at Letty Kellen. She was watching him intently, a mixture of anxiety and pride on her tan features. As he looked her lips came together and then parted, forming silent words that expressed her feelings for him. Jake nodded, smiled reassuringly, and stepped into the doorway.

"Now!" he called, and rushed into the open.

# ≈18≈

J<small>AKE</small> heard Letty and Cal Hollenbeck open up immediately. It seemed to take the Mexican soldiers and Fritz Benedict by surprise, for it was several moments before they came to life and laid down an answering fire. But Jake was wasting no time thinking about that. Once outside the way station, he fixed the location of the wagon in his mind, ducked low, and made a run for the vehicle.

He came first to the corral fence, where he paused. To climb over would immediately put him in full view of Melindrez and his men. Best to stay low as much as possible. Glancing along the board and pole fence, he spotted a wider space between two of the paralleling poles. Hurrying to the opening he squeezed through, then hunched low and doubled back to the wagon.

Keeping to the blind side of the vehicle, Benedict peered cautiously over the edge of the canvas-covered wagonbed. The soldiers were milling about as before, firing at will at the thick-walled way station. Melindrez, the Texan, and Fritz Benedict were still to the rear of the others, continuing to make certain none of the bullets coming from the ports of the stage stop would strike them. They were in close conversation, evidently working up some plan that would enable them to overcome the guns holding them at bay from inside the squat structure, and permit them to recover the wagon with its cargo of rifles and ammunition.

Moving carefully, Jake first untied the rope that linked

the nervous, fear-crazed bay gelding to the tailgate of the vehicle. He allowed the horse, whites of his eyes showing starkly, to break free. Head high, it trotted off toward the back of the corral.

Benedict turned then to the tarp. Lifting a side of it, he reached in and caught a corner of the crate that had burst open when the wagon overturned. Dragging it in close he removed three of the rifles, and then, on second thought, a fourth in the event one of the others failed to work. Coming about, and ducking low, he returned to the fence and laid the rifles on its opposite side.

Letty and Hollenbeck were shooting only occasionally now, Jake noted, and realized they were probably low on cartridges and were endeavoring to spread out their firing to make it last as long as possible. Immediately Jake returned to the wagon, and once again lifting the canvas, drew one of the boxes of cartridges to the side of the vehicle. Lifting it over the side of the bed, he carried it to where he had laid the rifles and placed the ammunition alongside the weapons.

It wasn't necessary now to drop back to the wide place in the corral fence; if Melindrez and the soldiers saw him it wouldn't matter. Thus, placing his hands on the top rail of the fence, Benedict vaulted over it to the opposite side.

Yells went up instantly. Jake flung a glance at the soldiers. Three of them were swinging wide, hoping to keep out of range of Hollenbeck and Letty's guns but still get near enough for a shot at him.

Jake bent low, scooped up the rifles, and ran to the rear door of the way station. Depositing them inside, he backtracked for the case of ammunition. The three soldiers who had cut away from the main body had reached the upper end of the corral, halted, and seemed at a loss as to what they should do next. Staying out of sight as much as possible, Benedict picked up the box of cartridges and hurried into the building.

The smoke haze had thickened and the pungent odor of burnt gunpowder was an irritant in his nostrils. Shards of glass from the shattered windows littered the floor, and the hammer of bullets against the front of the building was like a drumbeat.

Hollenbeck, out of ammunition, had already taken up one of the new rifles and was waiting for the cartridges. Letty was still using her weapon, her supply of bullets still holding out. Setting the box on the table, Benedict drew his skinning knife and pried back the lid.

"Help yourself!" he shouted to the station agent, noticing as he did the blood streaking the left side of the man's face. "You get hit?"

Hollenbeck shook his head as he feverishly began to load the magazine of the rifle. "Window glass. Dang stuff sort of went in every direction when a bullet smashed it."

Jake, brushing sand off the side of the rifle he had picked up and working its lever several times to be certain its action was clear, hastily began to feed shells into its magazine. Cal Hollenbeck, having crammed several hands full of ammunition into his pockets, had returned to the port near the doorway and was again pressing off regular shots at the soldiers.

Letty, her ammunition exhausted, turned and hurried

toward Jake. He saw her coming, and immediately handed her the weapon he had just loaded.

"Keep back from that port!" he warned.

Letty nodded and smiled. "I am—but you—I'm glad you're—"

"They're splitting up!" Hollenbeck called. "Looks like they're aiming to surround the place, try coming at us from all sides."

Jake, taking up one of the two remaining new guns and grabbing a handful of cartridges, crossed quickly to one of the openings in the walls. Three of the soldiers were galloping across the flat to join the trio at the upper end of the corral. Several others were moving toward the south end of the station, evidently intending to circle around to the rear of the building.

"I'll keep an eye on the wagon," Hollenbeck yelled. Crossing the smoky room in long strides, he made it to the back door. Throwing it open, he took up a position just inside where he could see anyone approaching the yard and the wagon.

Weapon ready, Jake took up the port vacated by the station agent. He wasn't particularly worried about the soldiers he'd seen circling to the lower end of the building; there were no windows or doors on that side they could rush.

Letty was back at her station now, discharging the new rifle with cool regularity. The weapon had a harder recoil than her own rifle, and each time the girl pressed off a shot, she flinched visibly.

Jake, his attention on a small group of soldiers being joined by Fritz Benedict, Melindrez, and the Texan, watched narrowly as the party began to move toward the station. Raising his weapon, Benedict waited out the moments until he knew the men were in range, and then drawing a bead on the nearest one, triggered a shot. The man jolted, rocked to one side, and fell to the ground. Jacking a fresh cartridge into the weapon's chamber, Jake threw another shot at one of the Mexicans cutting off and streaking for the corral. The bullet struck the man's saddle, and ricocheted off into the early morning air; but it did have a desired effect. The rider changed his mind about joining the soldiers at the upper end of the corral, and returned to Melindrez and the men with him.

The slowly advancing line halted as another man crumpled and fell limply from his horse. The soldiers hesitated, and began to wheel and move toward the Mexican colonel, still slightly to the rear with Fritz Benedict and the Texan.

"They turning tail?" Hollenbeck yelled.

"Not sure," Jake replied. "Backing off, that's for certain."

"How many did we get?"

"Four, maybe five."

"Still leaves a powerful lot of them out there," the station agent commented wryly. "Your pa still setting in his saddle?"

"Yeah, still is—"

Fritz Benedict was no longer riding double, Jake realized, but was now on a horse of his own. Evidently he had taken possession of a mount that had belonged to a dead or wounded soldier.

"They're coming over the fence!" Hollenbeck

yelled suddenly.

Jake spun. Motioning at Letty to stay at the port where she could continue shooting at Melindrez and the men with him while remaining comparatively safe, he hurried to the station agent's side. Hollenbeck, reloading, gestured toward the far corner of the fenced yard.

Four of the Mexicans had climbed over the top pole, and were dodging back and forth as they ran for the wagon. Jake leveled his rifle at the one in the lead and stopped him in midstride. Jacking a fresh cartridge into the weapon, he took careful aim at the next man in line and knocked him to the ground.

"Hell—the whole danged bunch are coming in!" Hollenbeck yelled.

Jake needed no warning of the fact. Standing well into the doorway, he was able to see the area fronting the building where Melindrez and the bulk of his men had formed a ragged line. But now, with no shooting coming from the way station when Letty was forced to stop and reload, the Colonel and his entire party, including Fritz Benedict and the Texan, were making a desperate run for the corral, and the wagon with its cargo of guns and ammunition.

Jake, steadying himself by leaning against the outer edge of the door frame, laid down a continuing fire against the oncoming soldiers. Hollenbeck, crouched beside him, was continuing to shoot at the men who had come over the fence.

The line of riders slowed, wavered briefly, and then came on—pointing straight for the gate to the corral. Once they had gained an entrance it would be next to impossible to save the guns and ammunition, Jake knew.

Abruptly Melindrez and his party began to veer off. The sound of gunfire increased—all coming from in front of the way station.

"It's the soldiers!" Letty Kellen cried, voice filled with relief. "They're here!"

Jake turned and hurried to a port in the front wall. Forrest and his men were driving straight at Melindrez and his soldiers. Several of the Mexicans were off their horses and one of the lieutenant's cavalrymen was down. But it was all Forrest's way; he had come in on Melindrez from the rear, and mounting a pronged charge, had caught the Mexican officer in a trap. Most of his men were already dead, and Melindrez himself, with a half dozen uniformed men, was riding hard for the protection of some brush off to the south.

Hollenbeck, laying his rifle on the table, moved to the front entrance and pulled open the door. Jake, still at the port, stared out over the slight incline where the fighting had taken place. Bodies were scattered about here and there, and several horses, saddles empty, waited patiently for riders who would not come. His father had been the cause of this, Jake thought bitterly; Fritz Benedict was a man who brought grief and unhappiness and death to all those who crossed his path.

"Forrest's coming back," he heard Hollenbeck say. "Looks like that colonel and what was left of his bunch got away."

Jake had turned and, with an arm about Letty, was walking slowly toward the door in the back of the room. He felt empty, let down, and somewhat at loose ends.

"Think I'd better take a look at my horse," he said. "Dragging him along behind that wagon like I did sort of set him—"

"Better hold up a minute," Hollenbeck called over his shoulder. "One of the lieutenant's boy's a'coming up fast. Maybe he wants to talk to you."

Jake and Letty hesitated. The cavalryman, a buck private, came off his horse and entered the room.

"Looking for Mr. Benedict—"

"Over there," the station agent said, pointing.

The young soldier crossed to where Jake stood. Touching the brim of his campaign hat, he said, "The lieutenant's compliments, sir. He said to tell you there were two civilians laying out there, one dead and the other'n dying. He thinks the one still alive is your pa, and figured maybe you'd like to talk to him before—"

The soldier broke off without finishing what he intended to say. Jake had turned away, was looking off in the direction of the corral.

"No need," he said. "I'm obliged to the lieutenant but I can't think of any reason to do what he suggests."

Benedict felt Letty's fingers tighten about his arm and glanced down. Her eyes were filled with concern.

"I think you should go, Jake," she said quietly. "Don't do something you may regret all your life."

Benedict gave that a long minute's thought. He had no wish to see his father, much less talk to him, but Letty seemed to think it important.

"All right," he said, nodding to the private, and holding on to Letty's hand, started for the door.

URIAL DETAILS were gathering up the bodies of the Mexican soldiers and carrying them off to a central point where they would later be taken care of. Other cavalrymen were rounding up the loose horses and leading them to the way station corral as Benedict, Letty and the station agent followed the young private to the slope where Forrest was waiting.

"You'll find three or four more of them Mex soldier boys in there," Jake heard Hollenbeck say to one of the blue-uniformed men moving by with two of the mounts he was taking to the fenced area. "And don't go forgetting them. I've done enough burying lately to last me for quite a spell."

Forrest was hunched between the prostrate bodies of the Texan and that of Fritz Benedict. When Jake and the others halted nearby, the officer came to his feet.

"Man there admits to the hijacking, and the murder of the two men. That's all I need to know for my report. Thought maybe you'd like to have a few last words with him. He hasn't got long."

Forrest waited for no comment from Jake, simply pivoted on a heel and, crossing to his horse, swung up into the saddle and rode toward the wagon in the corral, where he apparently intended to have a look at the salvaged rifles and ammunition.

Jake, features emotionless, no feeling of any kind coursing through him, looked down at the man who was his father. Fritz Benedict's brown suit was sweat-stained and caked with dust, and a broad stain of blood covered the front of his dirt-streaked shirt. Opening his eyes he stared up at Jake.

"Who the goddam hell you gawking at? Can't you let a man die in—"

"He's your son, Jake," Letty broke in, taking the awkward moment in hand. "Don't you remember him?"

"My kid? Hell, lady, I ain't got no kid—none that I know of, anyway."

Indifference abruptly vanished from Jake's attitude. Moving in closer he knelt beside the dying man.

"Ain't you Fritz Benedict?"

The man stirred, shook from a spasm of coughing. That over, he studied Jake closely as his wracked body quieted.

"I reckon you must be the boy Fritz talked about now and then. Last I heard you was somewhere running his farm."

A lightness was coursing through Jake. "Then you're not my pa—not Fritz Benedict?"

"No, I just took his name. Mine's Zack Rogers. Me and him was sort of partners. We got in a ruckus one night in a town up north of here—"

"Las Vegas?"

Rogers swallowed hard and brushed at his mouth. "Yeah, that was it. We got in this ruckus—was both a mite drunk. Somebody stuck a knife in Fritz, killed him dead—"

"So you took his name, and came on down here to go into raising horses—"

"Took his name all right. Had to. The law up Colorado

way was hunting me for another killing. Don't know nothing about horse-raising," Zack Rogers added, his words now dragging and barely audible. "Do recollect Fritz saying something about getting into it, but that's all. I come down here so's I'd be close to the border—to Mexico."

Rogers went into another coughing spell as Jake drew himself erect. Benedict felt as if the weight of the world had been lifted from his shoulders, and the expectation of a new, bright, and unclouded life had opened up for him. He glanced at Letty. The girl was smiling, and her eyes were soft and filled with happiness, equally glad that the shadow hovering about Jake was no longer there.

Jake nodded then to the grinning Cal Hollenbeck and looked down at Rogers. "Want to thank you—"

Rogers' slack features drew into a frown. "What the hell's that mean? Thank me for what?"

"For not being my pa, and for living long enough to tell me so."

Zack Rogers closed his eyes. "Ain't sure what you're getting at, and I reckon it don't matter none. Now," he added wearily, "I'll be mighty obliged if you'll get the hell away from here, and let me die in peace."

Forrest and his cavalrymen had gone, taking with them their wounded, the hijacked wagon with its load of guns and ammunition, the horses that had belonged to Melindrez' detachment, and the several Mexican soldiers who were now prisoners. Those followers of the colonel who had not survived the minor engagement, as the lieutenant termed it, were in a common grave well up on the slope.

"What will you do now?" Letty asked as Jake, sitting with her at the table in the way station's outsize kitchen, refilled her cup with coffee. The pot had been freshly brewed by Cal Hollenbeck, now out in the corral going about his regular duties.

"Go ahead with what I was planning to do—"

"Raise horses?"

Jake nodded, took a swallow of the strong, black liquid. "That's it. You be interested in being my partner?"

Letty smiled and considered him quizzically. "Are you asking me to marry you?"

"I reckon I am. Kind of hard to put it in fancy words, but—"

"It's not necessary, as long as I know what you mean. And I do!" Rising, Letty circled the table, and leaning over, kissed him soundly. "There, that seals it. We can ride into 'Cruces, find a preacher, and—"

"No," Jake cut in, shaking his head. "First off, we'll go tell your pa and get that part over with."

"Why bother?" Letty said, shrugging. "I doubt if it means anything to him. Anyway, he'll find out sooner or later."

"Maybe so, but I've got to know how he's going to feel about it. We'll be neighbors, and I won't have something hanging over our heads. We'll ride into town after we've seen him—"

"You won't have to go looking for him," Letty said, looking toward the station's entrance. "He's here—"

Jake got to his feet and faced the doorway. The portieres had been pulled aside and Tom Kellen, with several members of his crew behind him, was standing in the opening.

"Been hunting you," the rancher stated in a hard, flat voice to Letty. "Figured you'd got yourself in some real bad trouble. You all right? Benedict, damn you—if you've ruined my daughter I'll—"

Letty laughed, the sound a light, amused tinkling in the quiet room.

"I'm fine, Papa—and I haven't been ruined. Anyway, Jake and I are getting married."

"Married!" Kellen exploded. "I'll not let you throw your life away on a no-good, penniless saddlebum like him! He won't turn out no different from his pa—a renegade and a—"

"Hold on there, Tom," Hollenbeck interrupted from the doorway in the rear of the room. "You've got your ropes all crossed up. Fellow that done that hijacking wasn't Jake's pa. Now, let's you and me step out back, and I'll set you straight about a few things."

Kellen, face dark and frowning, walked stiffly by Letty and Jake and, joining the station agent, stepped out into the area behind the building.

Jake watched them until they had disappeared, and then turned to Letty. "Your pa knows about us now. Can't see no need to hang around here any longer," he said, putting his arms around the girl. "And I'm not anxious to see him eat crow. Every man's got a right to his pride."

Letty smiled up at him. "You're my kind of man, Jake

Benedict," she said, eyes shining. "Let's get our horses and head for Las Cruces—"

"And that preacher," Jake finished as they started for the door.

**Center Point Publishing**
600 Brooks Road ● PO Box 1
Thorndike ME 04986-0001 USA

(207) 568-3717

US & Canada:
1 800 929-9108